Algis Budrys is not simply an excellent writer: he has soul. And in this volume of cautionary tales he holds up a mirror to *Homo sapiens* – one of those warped funfair mirrors, admittedly, but the distortions only serve to make the images more recognizable. He portrays us in different moods and circumstances, but from each story emerges a view of human nature which is sympathetic without being wholly approving.

From Man's confrontation with aliens, mutants, androids – even himself – the author makes a plea for a little less arrogance: we are not even masters of ourselves, let alone whole galaxies.

All that *is* clear is that Algis Budrys is a master of his craft, a deft constructor of fictional Moebius strips, elegant stories whose dazzling twists have puzzling implications.

'Be thankful for a writer of the calibre of Algis Budrys, who is not content with simply letting his imagination run riot into the future – though he does that magnificently' – *Manchester Evening News*

THE FURIOUS FUTURE

ALGIS BUDRYS

QUARTET BOOKS LONDON

Published by Quartet Books Limited 1975
27 Goodge Street, London W1P 1FD

First published in Great Britain by Victor Gollancz Ltd 1964

ISBN 0 704 31198 4

Printed in Great Britain by
Hunt Barnard Printing Ltd, Aylesbury, Bucks

ACKNOWLEDGEMENTS

Silent Brother and *The Peasant Girl*, published in *Astounding Science Fiction*. Copyright © 1956 by Street and Smith Publications, Inc.

Lower Than Angels, *The Skirmisher* and *Between the Dark and the Daylight*, published in *Infinity Science Fiction*. Copyright © 1956, 1957, 1958 by Royal Publications, Inc.

And Then She Found Him, published in *Venture Science Fiction*. Copyright © 1957 by Fantasy House, Inc.

The Man Who Tasted Ashes, published in *If*. Copyright © 1957 by Quinn Publishing Co., Inc.

Contact Between Equals, published in *Venture Science Fiction*. Copyright © 1958 by Mercury Press, Inc.

Dream of Victory, published in *Amazing Science Fiction Stories*. Copyright © 1953 by Ziff-Davis Publishing Co.

To Damon Knight

INTRODUCTION

Well, this is a collection of stories by one man, namely somebody with the improbable name of Algis Budrys, and I assure you the author hopes you enjoy reading them, because I wrote them with that purpose in mind.

This collection is pretty well representative of my entire career as a science fiction writer, from 1952 to the present time. *Dream of Victory* is the first novelette I ever wrote, and *The Man who Tasted Ashes* is, I think, well representative of the kind of story I've been writing lately; if not that, then *The Skirmisher* or *Contact between Equals*. *Dream of Victory*, as I was writing it, seemed a free-wheeling piece of technical bedazzlement. Happily, most of the experimentation in it was elevated to more comprehensible levels by Howard Browne, the quietly competent editor who bought it and with his pencil made me look a little more mature than I really was. There is a certain temporary value to a young writer in coming on as a prose innovator and pyrotechnician; I think there is more for the reader and, in the course of time, more for the writer in letting the story speak for itself.

I do not want to belabor you too long with the hows and whyfors of my 'career'. Most people, I have noticed, couldn't care less who writes their entertainment for them, though those few who do care, care very deeply. I'd like to say something for that minority, and for the even smaller number of people who would like to write and who read this sort of introduction for clues to the secret of success—as I still do. I'd like to add that *The Peasant Girl*, *And Then She Found Him*, and *Silent Brother* were the kind of story that seemed to make the biggest impression on the critics when they were written, and that they certainly made me feel like a man of deep emotional perception while I was writing them.

Contemporary science fiction criticism seems to place a very high value on a certain approach to people which is labelled 'insight'. I would like it clearly understood that when I wrote these stories I felt the same way, and still do, but it seems to me equally true that you are not going to understand very much about a man or, by extension, all men, within the span of one short story or even one average-length novel. When I was quite young I read a great deal, with no discrimination, and made the mistake of trying to live as if life and fiction were one and the same thing. They aren't, of course—fiction is organized differently, and its people are only representations of people. I wouldn't want anyone believing even for a minute that there is really more in these stories than could be put into them by someone who was in his twenties when he wrote them. There may be some significance to them beyond their value as, I hope, intelligent entertainment. But if there is, it is only because the reader, too, has some understanding of people and their situation, and can use his perceptiveness to flesh out the structure of suggestions and allusions that appear in the course of my telling these stories.

One more specific reference to the contents of this book. *Between the Dark and the Daylight* is a variation on a theme. I cannot think of a story that could be written today that is not, in fact, a variation of some part of the body of fiction created by the generations of craftsman entertainers who have gone before and often well ahead of those of us who labor in that vineyard today. But this one was deliberate; it is, I think, one of the very few stories I have done that I did not feel was all mine while I was writing it. This is because Damon Knight, to whom this volume is dedicated for that and other reasons, had written a story called *The Avenger* which stuck in my mind for years, to the point where I had to tweezer it out or go mad. I have turned it a little on its side and sandpapered it some, I think; I know I have pointed it in a different direction, and the last time I asked Damon about it he seemed rather tickled by the whole notion, which permits me to tell you in all sincerity that it is, by my lights, one of my favorite stories no matter which of us wrote it.

And, as the last intrusion between yourself and the contents of this book, I should like to add that the version of *The Peasant Girl* appearing here is not quite the same as that appearing in any other edition; by a stroke of what I consider to be good fortune, a carbon of the original manuscript turned up recently, innocent of the editorial afterthoughts which I have always felt took some of the finish off.

A.J.B.

SILENT BROTHER

THE FIRST STARSHIP was home.

At first, the sight of the *Endeavor's* massive bulk on his TV screen held Cable's eager attention. At his first glimpse of the starship's drift to its mooring, alongside a berthing satellite, he'd felt the intended impression of human grandeur; more than most viewers, for he had a precise idea of the scale of size.

But the first twitch of ambiguity came as he watched the crew come out and cross to the Albuquerque shuttle on their suit jets. He knew those men: Dugan, who'd be impatient to land, as he'd been impatient to depart; Frawley, whose white hair would be sparsely tousled over his tight pink scalp; Snell, who'd have run to fat on the voyage unless he'd exercised like the very devil and fasted like a hermit; young Tommy Penn, who'd be unable to restrain his self-conscious glances into the cameras.

It was exactly those thoughts which dulled his vicarious satisfaction. He stayed in front of the set, watching through the afternoon, while the four men took off their suits and grouped themselves briefly for the still photographers, while they got past the advance guard of reporters into the shuttle's after compartment, and refused to speak for the video coverage.

It made no essential difference that Snell was lean and graceful, or that all four of them, Frawley and Penn included, were perfectly poised and unruffled. Perhaps it was a little more irritating that they were.

Endeavor's crew was stepping gracefully into history.

The cameras and Cable followed the four men out of the

shuttle and across the sun-drenched field at Albuquerque. Together they watched every trivial motion; Dugan's first cigarette in six months; Frawley's untied shoelace, which he repaired by casually stopping in the middle of the gangway and putting a leg on the railing; Tommy Penn giving a letter to a guard to mail.

Together with a billion other inhabitants of what was no longer Man's only planet, Cable looked into the faces of the President of the United States, of the United Nations Secretary General, of Premier Sobieski, and Marshal Siemens. Less than others, because he had a professional's residual contempt for eulogies, he heard what they had to say.

By nine or nine-thirty that night he had gathered the essential facts about the solar system of Alpha Centaurus. There were five planets, two of them temperate and easily habitable, one of them showing strong hints of extensive heavy metal ores. The trip had been uneventful, the stay unmarked by extraordinary incident. There was no mention of inhabitants.

There was also no mention of anything going wrong with the braking system, and that, perhaps, intensified the crook that had begun to bend one corner of Cable's thin mouth.

"You're welcome," he couldn't help grunting as Frawley described the smoothness of the trip and the simplicity of landing. That decelerating an object of almost infinite mass within a definitely finite distance was at all complicated didn't seem to be worthy of mention.

More than anything, it was the four men's unshakable poise that began to grate against him.

"Happens every day," he grunted at them, simultaneously telling himself he'd turned into a crabby old man at thirty-four, muttering spitefully at his friends for doing what he no longer could.

But that flash of insight failed to reappear when his part in *Endeavor's* development was lumped in with the "hard-working, dedicated men whose courage and brilliance made our flight possible." Applied to an individual, phrases like that were meaningful. Used like this, they covered everyone from the mess hall attendants to the man in charge of keeping the armadillos from burrowing under the barrack footings.

He snapped the set off with a peevish gesture. Perhaps, if he stayed up, the program directors, running out of fresh material at last, might have their commentators fill in with feature stuff like "amazing stride forward in electronics," "unified field theory," "five years of arduous testing on practical application to spaceship propulsion," and the like. Eventually, if they didn't cut back to the regular network shows first, they might mention his name. Somebody might even think it important that *Endeavor* had cost the total destruction of one prototype and the near-fatal crash of another.

But suddenly he simply wanted to go to bed. He spun his chair away from the set, rolled into the bedroom, levered himself up and pulled his way onto the bed. Taking his legs in his callused hands, he put them under the blankets, turned off the lights, and lay staring up at the dark.

Which showed and told him nothing.

He shook his head at himself. It was only twenty miles to the field from here. If he was really that much of a gloryhound, he could have gone. He was a dramatic enough sight. And, in all truth, he hadn't for a minute been jealous while the *Endeavor* was actually gone. It was just that today's panegyrics had been a little too much for his vanity to stave off.

He trembled on the brink of admitting to himself that his real trouble was the feeling that he'd lost all contact with the world. But only trembled, and only on the brink.

Eventually he fell asleep.

He'd slept unusually well, he discovered when he awoke in the morning. Looking at his watch, he saw it had only been about eight hours, but it felt like more. He decided to try going through the morning without the chair. Reaching over to the stand beside his bed, he got his braces and tugged them onto his legs. Walking clumsily, he tottered into the bathroom with his canes, washed his face, shaved, and combed his hair.

He'd forgotten to scrub his bridge last night. He took it out now and realized only after he did so that his gums, top and bottom, were sore.

"Oh, well," he told himself in the mirror, "we all have our cross to bear."

He decided to leave the bridge out for the time being. He never chewed with his front teeth anyway. Whistling "Sweet Violets" shrilly, he made his way back into the bedroom, where he carefully dressed in a suit, white shirt, and tie. He'd seen too many beat-up men who let themselves go to pot. Living alone the way he did made it even more important for him to be as neat as he could.

What's more, he told himself insidiously, the boys might drop over.

Thinking that way made him angry at himself. It was pure deception, because the bunch wouldn't untangle themselves out of the red tape and de-briefings for another week. That kind of wishful thinking could drift him into living on hungry anticipations, and leave him crabbed and querulous when they failed to materialize on his unreal schedule.

He clumped into the kitchen and opened the refrigerator with a yank of his arm.

That was something else to watch out for. Compensation was all well and good, but refrigerators didn't need all that effort to be opened. If he got into the habit of applying excessive arm-strength to everything, the day might come when he'd convince himself a man didn't need legs at all. That, too, was a trap. A man could get along without legs, just as a man could teach himself to paint pictures with his toes. But he'd paint better with finger dexterity.

The idea was to hang on to reality. It was the one crutch everybody used.

He started coffee boiling and went back out to the living room to switch on the TV.

That was another thing. He could have deliberately stopped and turned it on while on his way to the kitchen. But he'd never thought to save the steps before he'd crashed. More difficult? Of course it was more difficult now! But he needed the exercise.

Lift. Swing. Lock. Lean. Lift other leg. Swine, lock. Lean. Unlock other leg. Lift—

He cursed viciously at the perspiration going down his face.

And now the blasted set wouldn't switch on. The knob was loose. He looked more closely, leaning carfeully to one side in order to get a look at the set's face.

He had no depth perception, of course, but there was something strange about the dark square behind the plastic shield over the face of the tube.

The tube was gone. He grunted incredulously, but, now that his eye was accustomed to the dimmer light in this room, he could see the inside of the cabinet through the shield.

He pushed the cabinet away from the wall with an unexpected ease that almost toppled him. The entire set was gone. The antenna line dangled loosely from the wall. Only the big speaker, mounted below the chassis compartment, was still there.

First, he checked the doors and windows.

The two doors were locked from the inside, and the house, being air-conditioned, had no openable windows. He had only to ascertain that none of the panes had been broken or removed. Then he catalogued his valuables and found nothing gone.

The check was not quite complete. The house had a cellar. But before he was willing to go through that effort, he weighed the only other possibility in balance.

His attitude on psychiatry was blunt, and on psychology only a little less so. But he was a pragmatist; that is, he played unintuitive poker with success.

Because he was a pragmatist, he first checked the possibility that he'd had a mental lapse and forgotten he'd called to have the set taken out for repairs. Unlocking the front door, he got the paper off the step. A glance at the date and a story lead beginning "Yesterday's return of the *Endeavor*—" exploded that hypothesis, not to his surprise. The set had been there last night. It was still too early today for any repair shop to be open.

Ergo, he had to check the cellar windows. He hadn't lost a day, or done anything else incredible like that. Tossing the paper on the kitchen table, he swung his way to the cellar door, opened it, and looked down, hoping against hope that he'd see the broken window from here and be able to report the burglary without the necessity of having to ease himself down the steps.

But, no such luck. Tucking the canes under his left arm, he grasped the railing and fought his body's drag.

Once down, he found it unnecessary to look at the windows. The set chassis was in the middle of his old, dust-covered workbench. It was on its side, and the wiring had been ripped out. The big tube turned its pale face toward him from a nest of other components. A soldering iron balanced on the edge of the bench, and some rewiring had been begun on the underside of the chassis.

It was only then—and this, he admitted to himself without any feeling of self-reproach, was perfectly normal for a man like himself—that he paid any notice to the superficial burns, few in number, on the thumb and forefinger of his left hand.

The essence of anything he might plan, he decided, was in discarding the possibility of immediate outside help.

He sat in his chair, drinking a cup of the coffee he'd made after having to scrape the burnt remains of the first batch out of the coffee-maker, and could see where that made the best sense.

He had no burglary to report, so that took care of the police. As for calling anyone else, he didn't have the faintest idea of whom to call if he'd wanted to. There was no government agency, local, state, or federal—certainly not international, ramified though the United Nations was—offering advice and assistance to people who disassembled their own TV sets in their sleep and then proceeded to re-work them into something else.

Besides, this was one he'd solve for himself.

He chuckled. What problem wasn't? He was constitutionally

incapable of accepting anyone else's opinion over his own, and he knew it.

Well, then, data thus far:

One ex-TV set in the cellar. Better: one collection of electronic parts.

Three burns on fingertips. Soldering iron?

He didn't know. He supposed that, if he ever took the trouble to bone up with a book or two on circuitry, he could throw together a fair FM receiver, and, given a false start or two, mock up some kind of jackleg video circuit. But he'd never used a soldering iron in his life. He imagined the first try might prove disgracefully clumsy.

Questions:

How did one shot-up bag of rag-doll bones and twitchless nerves named Harvey Cable accomplish all this in his sleep?

How did he pull that set out of the cabinet, hold it in both arms as he'd have to, and, even granting the chair up to this point, make it down the cellar steps?

Last question, par value, $64.00: Where had the tools come from?

He searched the house again, but there was definitely no one else in it.

Toward noon he found his mind still uneasy on one point. He got out his rubber-stamp pad, inked his fingertips, and impressed a set of prints on a sheet of paper. With this, his shaving brush, and a can of talcum powder, he made his way into the cellar again and dusted the face of the picture tube. The results were spotty, marred by the stiffness of the brush and his lack of skill, but after he hit on the idea of letting the powder drift across the glass like a dry ripple riding the impetus of his gently blown breath, he got a clear print of several of his fingers. There were some very faint prints that were not his own, but he judged from their apparent age that they must belong to the various assemblers in the tube's parent factory. There were no prints of comparable freshness to his own, and he knew he'd never handled the tube before.

That settled that.

Next, he examined the unfamiliar tools that had been laid on the bench. Some of them were arranged in neat order, but others—the small electric soldering iron, a pair of pliers, and several screwdrivers—were scattered among the parts. He dusted those, too, and found his own prints on them. All of the tools were new, and unmarked with work scratches.

He went over to where his electric drill was hanging up beside his other woodworking tools. There were a few shavings of aluminium clinging to the burr of the chuck. Going back to the reworked chassis, he saw that several new cuts and drillings had been made in it.

Well. He looked blankly at it all.

Next question: What in the name of holy horned hell am I building?

He sat looking thoughtfully down at the paper, which he'd finally come around to reading. He wasn't the only one infested with mysteries.

The story he'd glanced at before read:

OFFICAL CENSORSHIP SHROUDS
ENDEAVOR CREW

Albuquerque, May 14—*Yesterday's return of the* Endeavor *brought with it a return of outmoded press policies on the part of all official government agencies concerned. In an unprecedented move, both the U.S. and U.N. Press Secretaries late last night refused to permit further interviews with the crew or examination of the starship. At the same time, the Press was restricted to the use of official mimeographed releases in its stories.*

Unofficial actions went even farther. Reporters at the Sandia auxiliary press facilities were told "off the record" that a "serious view" might "well be taken" if attempts were made to circumvent these regulations. This was taken to mean that offending newspapers would henceforth be cut off from all official releases. Inasmuch as these releases now constitute all the available information on the Endeavor, *her crew, and their discoveries, this "unofficial advice" is tantamount to a threat of total censorship. The spokesman giving this "advice" declined to let his name be used.*

Speculation is rife that some serious mishap, in the nature of an unsuspected disease or infection, may have been discovered among members of the Endeavor's *crew. There can, of course, be no corroboration or denial of this rumor until the various agencies involved deign to give it.*

Under this was a box: *See Editorial, "A Free Press in a Free World," p. 23.*

Cable chuckled, momentarily, at the paper's discomfiture. But his face twisted into a scowl again while he wondered whether Dugan, Frawley, Snell, and Tommy Penn were all right. The odds were good that the disease theory was a bunch of journalistic hogwash, but anything that made the government act like that was sure to be serious.

Some of his annoyance, he realized with another chuckle on a slightly different note, came from his disappointment. It looked like it might be even longer before the bunch was free to come over and visit him.

But this return to yesterday's perverse selfishness did not stay with him long. He was looking forward eagerly to tonight's experiment. Cable smiled with a certain degree of animation as he turned the pages. By tomorrow he'd have a much better idea of what was happening here. Necessarily, his own problem eclipsed the starship mystery. But that was good.

It was nice, having a problem to wrestle with again.

There was an item about a burgled hardware store—"small tools and electrical supplies were taken"—and he examined it coolly. Data on source of tools?

The possibility existed. Disregard the fact he was the world's worst raw burglar material. He hadn't been a set designer before last night, either.

He immediately discarded the recurring idea that the police should be called. They'd refuse to take him seriously; there was even a tangible risk of being cross-questioned by a psychiatrist.

He judged as objectively as he could that it would take several days of this before he grew unreasonably worried. Until such time, he was going to tackle this by himself, as best he could.

His gums still ached, he noticed—more so than this morning, perhaps.

His eyes opened, and he looked out at morning sunshine. So, he hadn't been able to keep awake at night. He'd hardly expected to.

Working methodically, he looked at the scratch pad on which he'd been noting the time at ten-minute intervals. The last entry, in a sloppy hand, was for eleven-twenty. Somewhat later than he was usually able to keep awake, but not significantly much.

He looked at his watch. It was now 7:50 a.m. A little more than eight hours, all told, and again he felt unusually rested. Well, fine. A sound mind in a sound body, and all that. The early worm gets the bird. Many lights make hand work easier on the eyes. A nightingale in the bush is worth two birds in the hand.

He was also pretty cheerful.

Strapping on his braces and picking up his canes, he now swung himself over to the locked bedroom door. There were no new burns on his fingers. He looked at the door critically. It was still locked, and, presumably until proven otherwise, the key was still far out of reach in the hall, where he'd skittered it under the door after turning the lock.

He turned back to the corner where he'd left the screwdriver balanced precariously on a complex arrangement of pots and pans which the tool's weight kept from toppling, and which he'd had to hold together with string while he was assembling it. After placing the screwdriver, he'd burned the string, as well as every other piece of twine or sewing thread in the house.

He was unable to lift the tool now without sending the utensils tumbling with a crash and clatter that made him wince. It seemed only reasonable that the racket would have been quite capable of waking the half-dead, even if none of his other somnambulistic activities had. But the screwdriver hadn't been touched—or else his sleeping brain was more ingenious than his waking one.

Well, we'll see. He went back to the door, found no scratches on the lock, but left quite a few in the process of taking the lock apart and letting himself out.

Data: key still far out on hall floor. He picked it up after some maneuvering with his canes and brace locks, put it in his pocket, and went to the cellar door, which was also still locked.

His tactics here had been somewhat different. The key was on the kitchen table, on a dark tablecloth, with flour scattered over it in a random pattern he'd subsequently memorized with no hope of being able to duplicate it.

The flour was undisturbed. Nevertheless, there was a possibility he might have shaken out the cloth, turned it over to hide the traces of flour remaining, replaced the key, and somehow duplicated the flour pattern—or, at any rate, come close enough to fool himself, provided he was interested in fooling himself.

This checked out negative. He'd done no such thing. He defied anyone to get all the traces of flour out of the cloth without laundering it, in which case he'd been wonderfully ingenious at counterfeiting several leftover food stains.

Ergo, he hadn't touched the key. *Ipso facto. Reductio ad absurdum. Non lessi illegitimis te carborundum.*

Next move.

He unlocked the cellar door and lowered himself down the steps.

Which gave him much food for thought. He stood cursing softly at the sight of the chassis with more work done on it.

For the first time he felt a certain degree of apprehension. No bewilderment, as yet; too many practical examples in his lifetime had taught him that today's inexplicable mystery was tomorrow's dry fact. Nevertheless, he clumped forward with irritated impatience and stood looking down at the workbench.

All the tools were scattered about now. The tube had been

wiped clean of his amateur fingerprintings yesterday, and the tools, apparently, had come clean in handling. The chassis was tipped up again, and some parts, one of which looked as though it had been revamped, had been bolted to its upper surface and wired into the growing circuit. The soldering was much cleaner; apparently he was learning.

He was also learning to walk through locked doors, damn it!

He'd left a note for himself: "What am I doing?" block-printed in heavy letters on a shirt cardboard he'd propped against the chassis. It had been moved to one side, laid down on the far end of the bench.

There was no answer.

He glowered down at the day's paper, his eye scanning the lines, but not reading. It wasn't even in focus.

His entire jaw was aching, but he grimly concentrated past that, grinding at the situation with the sharp teeth of his mind.

The new fingerprints on the set were his, again. He was still doing a solo—or was it a duet with himself?

He rechecked the locks, examined the doors, tried to move the immovable hinge pins, and even tested the bedroom and cellar windows to make sure against the absurd possibility that he'd gotten them open and clambered in and out that way.

The answer was no.

But the thing in the cellar had more work done on it.

The answer was yes.

That led nowhere. Time out to let the subconscious mull it over. He concentrated on the paper, focusing his blurred vision on the newspaper by main force, wondering how the starship base was doing with *its* mystery.

Not very well. The entire base had been quarantined, and the official press releases cut to an obfuscatory trickle.

For the moment, his anxiety about the boys made him forget his preoccupation. Reading as rapidly as he could with his foggy eye, he discovered that the base was entirely off limits to anyone now; apparently that applied to government personnel, too.

The base had been cordoned off by National Guard units at a distance of two miles. The paper was beating the disease drum for all it was worth, and reporting a great deal of international anxiety on the subject.

It seemed possible now that the paper was correct in its guess. At any rate, it carried a front-page story describing the sudden journeys of several top-flight biologists and bio-chemists en route to the base, or at least this general area.

Cable clamped his lips into a worried frown.

He'd been in on a number of the preliminary briefings on the trip, before he'd disqualified himself. The theory had been that alien bugs wouldn't be any happier on a human being than, say, a rock lichen would be. But even the people quoting the theory had admitted that the odds were not altogether prohibitive against it, and it was Cable's experience that theories were only good about twenty-five per cent of the time in the first place.

It was at this point that the idea of a correlation between the starship's mystery and his own first struck him.

He fumed over it for several hours.

The idea looked silly. Even at second or third glance, it resembled the kind of brainstorm a desperate man might get in a jam like this.

That knowledge alone was enough to prejudice him strongly against the possibility. But he couldn't quite persuade himself to let go of it.

Item: The crew of the starship might be down with something.

Item: The base was only twenty miles away. Air-borne infection?

Item: The disease, if it was a disease, had attacked the world's first astronauts. By virtue of his jouncings-about in the prototype models, he also qualified as such.

A selective disease attacking people by occupational speciality?

Bushwah!

Air-borne infection in an air-conditioned house?

All right, his jaw ached and his vision was blurred.

He pawed angrily at his eye.

When he had conceived of interfering with the progress of the work, he'd intended it as one more cool check on what the response would be. But now it had become something of a personal spite against whatever it was he was doing in the cellar.

By ten o'clock that night, he'd worked himself into a fuming state of temper. He clumped downstairs, stood glaring at the set, and was unable to deduce anything new from it. Finally he followed the second part of his experimental program by ripping all the re-done wiring loose, adding a scrawled "Answer me!" under yesterday's note, and went to bed seething. Let's see what he did about *that*.

His mouth ached like fury in the morning, overbalancing his sense of general well-being. He distracted himself with the thought that he was getting a lot of sound rest, for a man on a twenty-four hour day, while he lurched quickly into the bathroom and peeled his lips back in front of the mirror.

He stared at the front of his mouth in complete amazement. Then he began to laugh, clutching the washbasin and continuing to look incredulously at the sight in the mirror.

He was teething!

With the look of a middle-aged man discovering himself with chicken pox, he put his thumb and forefinger up to his gums and felt the hard ridges of outthrusting enamel.

He calmed down with difficulty, unable to resist the occasional fresh temptation to run his tongue over the sprouting teeth. Third sets of teeth occasionally happened, he knew, but he'd dismissed that possibility quite early in the game. Now, despite his self-assurances at the time the bridge was fitted, he could admit that manufactured dentures were never as satisfying as the ones a man grew for himself. He grinned down at the pronged monstrosity he'd been fitting into his mouth each morning for the past year, picked it up delicately, and dropped it into the waste basket with a satisfying sound.

Whistling again for the first time in two days, he went out to the cellar door and opened it, bent, and peered down. He grunted and reached for the rail as he swung his right foot forward.

He opened his mouth in a strangled noise of surprise. He'd seen *depth* down those stairs. His other eye was working again—the retina had re-attached itself!

The stairs tumbled down with a crash as their supports, sawed through, collapsed under his weight. The railing came limply loose in his clutch, and he smashed down into the welter of splintered boards ten feet below.

I shouldn't, he thought to himself in one flicker of consciousness have ripped up that set. Then he pitched into blackness again.

He rolled over groggily, wiped his hand over his face, and opened his eyes. There didn't seem to be any pain.

He was facing the stairs, which had been restored. The braces had been splinted with scrap lumber, and two of the treads were new wood. The old ones were stacked in a corner, and he half-growled at the sight of brown smears on their splintered ends.

There was still no pain. He had no idea of how long he'd been lying there on the cellar floor. His watch was smashed.

He looked over at the workbench, and saw that whatever he'd been building was finished. The chassis sat right side up on the bench, the power cord trailing up to the socket.

It looked like no piece of equipment he'd ever seen. The tube was lying on the bench beside the chassis, wired in but unmounted. Apparently it didn't matter whether it was rigidly positioned or not. He saw two control knobs rising directly out of the top of the chassis, as well as two or three holes in the chassis where components had been in the TV circuit but were not required for this new use. The smaller tubes glowed. The set was turned on.

Apparently, too, he hadn't cared what condition his body was in while he worked on it.

He'd been fighting to keep his attention away from his

body. The teeth and the eye had given him a hint he didn't dare confirm at first.

But it was true. He could feel the grittiness of the floor against the skin of his thighs and calves. His toes responded when he tried to move them, and his legs flexed.

His vision was perfect, and his teeth were full-grown, strong and hard as he clamped them to keep his breathing from frightening him.

Something brushed against his leg, and he looked down. His leg motions had snapped a hair-thin copper wire looped around one ankle and leading off toward the bench. He looked up, and the triggered picture tube blinked a light in his eyes.

Blink can't *think* blink rhythm I *think* blink trick think *blink* sink blink *wink*—CAN'T *THINK*!

He slammed his hands up against his face, covering his eyes.

He held them there for a few choked moments. Then he opened two fingers in a thin slit, like a little boy playing peek-a-boo with his mother.

The light struck his eye again. This time there was no getting away. The trigger of the picture tube's flicker chipped at each attempt to think, interrupting each beat of his brain as it tried to bring its attention on anything but the stimulus of that blink. He had no chance of even telling his hands to cover his eyes again.

His body collapsed like a marionette, and his face dropped below the flickering beam. His head hanging, he got to his hands and knees like a young boy getting up to face the schoolyard bully again.

The blink reflected off the floor and snapped his head up like a kick. The beam struck him full in the eyes.

It was even impossible for him to tell his throat to scream. He swayed on his knees, and the blink went into his brain like a sewing machine.

Eventually he fell again, and by now he was beginning to realize what the machine was doing to him. Like an Air Force cadet feeling the controls of his first trainer, he began to realize that there was a logic to this—that certain actions produced a certain response—that the machine could predict the rhythm of his thoughts and throttle each one as it tried to leave his brain and translate itself into coherent thought.

He looked up deliberately, planning to snatch his face to one side the moment he felt it grip him again.

This time he was dimly aware of his arms, flailing upward and trying to find his face in a hopelessly unco-ordinated effort.

He discovered he could sidestep the blink. If he upset the machine's mechanical prediction, he could think. His mind rolled its thought processes along well-worn grooves. As simple a thought as knowing he was afraid had to search out its correlations in a welter of skin temperature data, respiration and heartbeat notations, and an army of remembered precedents.

If he could reshuffle that procedure, using data first that would ordinarily claim his attention last, he could think. The blink couldn't stop him.

Like a man flying cross-country for the first time, he learned that railroads and highways are snakes, not arrows. Like a pilot teaching his instincts to push the nose *down* in a stall, abrogating the falling-response that made him ache to pull back on the stick, he learned. He had to, or crash.

To do that, he had to change the way he thought.

The blink turned into a flashing light that winked on and off at pre-set intervals. He reached up and decided which knob was logically the master switch. He turned it off, feeling the muscles move, his skin stretch, and his bones roll to the motion. He felt the delicate nerves in his fingertips tell him how much pressure was on his capillaries, and the nerves under his fingernails corroborate their reading against the pressure there. His fingers told him when the switch was off, not the click of it. There was no click. The man who'd put that switch in hadn't intended it for human use.

Most of all, he felt his silent brother smile within him.

The three uniformed men stopped in the doorway and stared at him.

"Harvey Cable?" one of them finally asked. He blinked his eyes in the bright sunshine, peering through the doorway.

Cable smiled. "That's right. Come on in."

The man who'd spoken wore an Air Force major's insignia and uniform. The other two were United Nations inspectors. They stepped in gingerly, looking around them curiously.

"I refurnished the place," Cable said pleasantly. "I've got a pretty good assortment of wood-working tools in the cellar."

The major was pale, and the inspectors were nervous. They exchanged glances. "Typical case," one of them muttered, as though it had to be put in words.

"We understood you were crippled," the major stated.

"I was, Major—?"

"Paulson. Inspector Lee, and Inspector Carveth." Paulson took a deep breath. "Well, we're exposed, now. May we sit down?"

"Sure. Help yourselves. Exposed to the disease, you mean?"

The major dropped bitterly into a chair, an expression of surprise flickering over his face as he realized how comfortable it was. "Whatever it is. Contagious psychosis, they're saying now. No cure," he added bluntly.

"No disease," Cable said, but made little impression. All three men had their mouths clamped in thin, desperate lines. Apparently the most superficial contact with the "disease" had proved sufficient for "infection."

"Well," Cable said, "what can I do for you? Would you like a drink first?"

Paulson shook his head, and the inspectors followed suit. Cable shrugged politely.

"We came here to do a job," Paulson said doggedly. "We might as well do it." He took an envelope out of his blouse pocket. "We had quite a battle with the Postmaster General about this. But we got it. It's a letter to you from Thomas Penn."

Cable took it with a wordless tilt of one eyebrow. It had been opened. Reaching into the envelope, he pulled out a short note:

Harv—

Chances are, this is the only way we'll have time to get in touch with you. Even so, you may not get it. Don't worry about us, no matter what you hear. We're fine. You won't know how fine until you get acquainted with the friend we're sending you.

Good luck,
Tommy

He smiled, feeling his silent brother smile, too. For a moment they shared the warmth of feeling between them. Then he turned his attention back to the three men. "Yes?"

Paulson glared at him. "Well, what about it? What friend? Where is he?"

Cable grinned at him. Paulson would never believe him if he told him. So there was no good in telling him. He'd have to find out for himself.

Just as everybody would. There was no logic in telling. Telling proved nothing, and who would welcome a "parasitic" alien into his body and mind, even if that "parasite" was a gentle, intelligent being who kept watch over the host, repairing his health, seeing to his well-being? Even if that "parasite" gave you sanity and rest, tranquillity and peace, because he needed it in order to fully be your brother? Who wants symbiosis until he's felt it? Not you, Major. Not Harvey Cable, either, fighting his battles on the edge of the world, proud, able —but alone.

Who wants to know any human being can go where he wants to, do what he wants to, now? Who wants to know disease is finished, age is calm, and death is always a falling asleep, now? Not the medical quacks, not the lonely hearts bureaus, not the burial insurance companies. Not the people who live on fear. Who wants a brother who doesn't hesitate to slap you down if you need it while you're growing up?

Should the *Endeavor* have brought riot and war back with it? Better a little panic now, damping itself out before it even gets out of the Southwest.

No, you don't tell people about this. You simply give it.

"Well?" Paulson demanded again.

Cable smiled at him. "Relax, Major. There's all the time in the world. My friend's where you can't ever get him unless I let you. What's going on up around the base?"

Paulson grunted his anger. "I don't know," he said harshly. "We were all in the outer quarantine circle."

"The outer circle. It's getting to one circle after another, is it?"

"Yes!"

"What's it like? The disease. What does it do?"

"You know better than I do."

"Men walking in their sleep? Doing things? Getting past guards and sentries, getting out of locked rooms? Some of them building funny kinds of electronic rigs?"

"What do you think?" Paulson was picturing himself doing it. It was plain on his face.

"I think so. Frighten you?"

Paulson didn't answer.

"It shouldn't. It's a little rough, going it alone, but with others around you, I don't imagine you'll have any trouble."

It wasn't the man who momentarily disorganized his body and passed under a door who was frightened. Not after he could do it of his own volition instead of unconsciously, at his brother's direction. It was the man who watched him do it, just as it was the men on the ground who were terrified for the Wright brothers. Paulson was remembering what he'd seen. He had no idea of how it felt to be free.

Cable thought of the stars he'd seen glimmering as he rode *Endeavor's* prototype, and the curtains and clouds of galaxies beyond them. He'd wanted to go to them all, and stand on every one of their planets.

Well, he couldn't quite have that. There wasn't time enough in a man's life. But his brother, too, had been a member of a race chained to one planet. The two of them could see quite a bit before they grew too old.

So we were born in a Solar System with one habitable planet, and we developed the star drive. And on Alpha's planet, a race hung on, waiting for someone to come along and give it hands and bodies.

What price the final plan of the universe? Will my brother and I find the next piece of the ultimate jigsaw puzzle?

Cable looked at the three men, grinning at the thought of the first time one of them discovered a missing tooth was growing back in.

Starting with Paulson, he sent them each a part of his brother.

BETWEEN THE DARK AND THE DAYLIGHT

A CURVED SECTION of the dome, twenty feet thick with the stubs of reinforcing rod rusty and protruding through the dampmarked concrete, formed the ceiling and back wall of Brendan's office. There was a constant drip of seepage and condensation. Near the mildew-spotted floor, a thin white mist drifted in torn swirls while the heating coils buried in the concrete fought back against the cold. There was one lamp in the windowless dark, a glowing red coil on Brendan's desk, well below the eye level of the half-dozen men in the room. The heavy office door was swung shut, the locking bars pushed home. If it had not been, there would have been some additional light from the coils in the corridor ceiling, outside the office. Brendan would have had to face into it, and the men in the front of him would have been looming shadows to him.

But the door was shut, as Brendan insisted it must be, as all doors to every room and every twenty-foot length of corridor were always shut as much of the time as possible—at Brendan's insistence—as though the dome were a sinking ship.

Conducted by the substance of the dome, there was a constant *chip, chip, chip* coming from somewhere, together with a heartless gnawing sound that filled everyone's head as though they were all biting on sandpaper.

Brendan growled from behind his desk: "I'm in charge."

The five men on the opposite side of the desk had tacitly chosen Falconer for their spokesman. He said: "But we've all got something to say about it, Brendan. You're in charge, but nothing gives you the power to be an autocrat."

"No?"

"Nothing. The Expedition Charter, in fact, refers to a Board of Officers—"

"The Expedition Charter was written four hundred years ago, a thousand lightyears away. The men who drew it up are dust. The men who signed it are dust."

"You're in the direct line of descent from the first Captain."

"Then you're recognizing me as a hereditary monarch, Falconer. I don't see the basis of your complaint."

Falconer—lean as a whip from the waist down, naked, thick-torsoed, covered with crisp, heavy fur—set his clawed feet a little apart and thrust out his heavy underjaw, clearing his sharp canine tusks away from his flat lips. He lifted his enormous forearms out from his sides and curved his fingers. "Don't pare cheese with us, Brendan. The rest of the dome might be willing to let it go, as long as things're so near completion. But not us. We won't stand for it." The men with him were suddenly a tense pack, waiting, ready.

Brendan stood up, a member of Falconer's generation, no more evolved than any of them. But he was taller than Falconer or any other man in the room. He was bigger, his cruelly-shaped jaw broader, his tusks sharper, his forearm muscles out of all proportion to the length of the bone, like clubs. His eyes burned out from under his shaggy brows, lambent with the captive glow of the lighting coil, set far back under the protection of heavy bone. The slitted nostrils of his flat nose were suddenly flared wide.

"You don't dare," he rumbled. His feet scraped on the floor. "I'll disembowel the first man to reach me." He lashed out and sent the massive bronze desk lurching aside, clearing the way between himself and Falconer's party. And he waited, while the other men sent sidelong glances at Falconer and Falconer's eyes slowly fell. Then Brendan grunted. "This is why I'm in charge. Charters and successions don't mean a thing after four hundred years. Not if a good man goes against them. You'll keep on taking my orders."

"What kind of paranoiac's world do you live in?" Falconer said bitterly. "Imposing your will on all of us. Doing everything your way and no other. We're not saying your methods are absolutely going to wreck the project, but—"

"What?"

"We've all got a stake in this. We've all got children in the nursery, the same way you do."

"I don't favor my son over any of the others. Get that idea out of your head."

"How do we know? Do we have anything to do with the nursery? Are we allowed inside?"

"I'm this generation's biotechnician and pedagogical specialist. That's the Captain's particular job. That's the way it's been since the crash—by the same tradition you were quoting—and that's the way it has to be. This is a delicate business. One amateur meddling in it can destroy everything we're doing and everything that was done in the past. And we'll never have another chance."

"All right. But where's the harm in looking in on them? What's your point in not letting us at the cameras?"

"They're being overhauled. We're going to need to have them in perfect working order tomorrow, when we open the nursery gates to the outside. That's when it'll be important to look in on the children and make sure everything's all right."

"And meanwhile only you can get into the nursery and see them."

"That's my job."

"Now, listen, Brendan, we all went through the nursery, too. And your father had the same job you do. We weren't sealed off from everybody but him. We saw other people. You know that just as well as we do."

Brendan snorted. "There's no parallel. We weren't the end

product. We were just one more link in the chain, and we had to be taught all about the dome, because the hundred-odd of us were going to constitute its next population. We had to be taught about the air control system, the food distribution, the power plant—and the things it takes to keep this place functioning as well as it can. We had to each learn our job from the specialist who had it before us.

"But the next generation isn't going to need that. That's obvious. This is what we've all been working for. To free them. Ten generations ago, the first of us set out to free them.

"And that's what I'm going to do, Falconer. That's my job, and nobody here could do it, but me, in my way."

"They're our children too!"

"All right, then, be proud of them. Tomorrow they go outside, and there'll be men out on the face of this world at last. Your flesh, your blood, and they'll take this world away from the storms and the animals. That's what we've spent all this time for. That's what generations of us have huddled in here for, hanging on for this day. What more do you want?"

"Some of the kids are going to die," one of the other men growled. "No matter how well they're equipped to handle things outside, no matter how much has been done to get them ready. We don't expect miracles from you, Brendan. But we want to make sure you've done the best possible. We can't just twiddle our thumbs."

"You want work to do? There's plenty. Shut up and listen to what's going on outside."

The gnawing filled their heads. Brendan grinned coldly. And the chipping sound, which had slowed a little, began a rapid pace again.

"They just changed shifts," Brendan said. "One of them got tired and a fresh one took over."

"They'll never get through to us in the time they've got left," Falconer said.

"No?" Brendan turned on him in rage. "How do you know? Maybe they've stopped using flint. Maybe they've got hold of something like diamonds. What about the ones that just use their teeth? Maybe they're breeding for tusks that concrete won't wear down. Think we've got a patent on that idea? Think because we do it in a semi-automatic nursery, blind evolution can't do it out in that wet hell outside?"

Lusic—the oldest of them there, with sparse fur and lighter jaws, with a round skull that lacked both a sagittal crest and a bone shelf over the eyes—spoke for the first time.

"None of those things seem likely," he said in a voice muffled by the air filter his generation had to wear in this generation's ecology. "They are possibilities, of course, but only that. These are not purposeful intelligences like ourselves. These are only immensely powerful animals—brilliant, for animals, in a world lacking a higher race to cow them—but they do not lay plans. No, Brendan, I don't think your attempt to distract us has much logic in it. The children will be out, and will have destroyed them, before there can be any real danger to the dome's integrity. I can understand your desire to keep us busy, because we are all tense as our efforts approach a climax. But I do think your policy is wrong. I think we should long ago have been permitted a share in supervising the nursery. I think your attempt to retain dictatorial powers is an unhealthy sign. I think you're afraid of no longer being the most powerful human being in our society. Whether you know it or not, I think that's what's behind your attitude. And I think something ought to be done about it, even now."

"*Distract!*" Brendan's roar made them all retreat. He marched slowly toward Lusic, and the other man began to back away. "When I need advice from a sophist like you, that'll be the time when we all need distraction!" He stopped when Lusic was pressed against the wall, and he pointed at the wall.

"There is nothing in this world that loves us. There is nothing in this world that can even tolerate us. Generations of us have lived in this stone trap because not one of us—not even I—could live in the ecology of this planet. It was never made for men. Men could not have evolved on it. It would have killed them when they crawled from the sea, killed them when they tried to breathe its atmosphere, killed them when they tried to walk on its surface, and when they tried to take a share of food away from the animals that *could* evolve here. We are a blot and an abomination upon it. We are weak, loathsome grubs on its iron face. And the animals know us for what we are. They may even guess what we have spent generations in becoming, but it doesn't matter whether they do or not—they hate us, and they won't stop trying to kill us.

"When the expedition crashed here, they were met by storms and savagery. They had guns and their kind of air regenerators and a steel hull for shelter, and still almost all of them died. But if they had been met by what crowds around this dome today, they would never have lived at all, or begun this place.

"You're right, Lusic—there are only animals out there. Animals that hate us so much, some of them have learned to hold stones in their paws and use them for tools. They hate us so much they chip, chip, chip away at the dome all day, and gnaw at it, and howl in the night for us to come out, because they hate us so.

"We only *hope* they won't break through. We can only hope the children will drive them away in time. We don't know. But you'd rather be comfortable in your hope. You'd rather come in here and quibble at my methods. But I'm not your kind. Because if I don't know, I don't hope. I act. And because I act, and you don't, and because I'm in charge, you'll do what I tell you."

He went back to his desk and shoved it back to its place. "That's all. I've heard your complaint, and rejected it. Get back to work reinforcing the dome walls. I want that done."

They looked at him, and at each other. He could see the indecision on their faces. He ignored it, and after a moment they decided for retreat. They could have killed him, acting together, and they could have acted together against any other man in the dome. But not against him. They began going out.

Lusic was the last through the door. As he reached to pull it shut, he said, "We may kill you if we can get enough help."

Brendan looked at his watch and said quietly: "Lusic—it's the twenty-fifth day of Kislev, on Chaim Weber's calendar. Stop off at his place and tell him it's sunset, will you?"

He waited until Lusic finally nodded, and then ignored him again until the man was gone.

When his office door was locked, he went to the television screen buried in the wall behind him, switched it on, and looked out at the world outside.

Rain—rain at a temperature of 1° Centigrade—blurred the camera lenses, sluicing over them, blown up through the protective baffles, giving him not much more than glutinous light and shadow to see. But Brendan knew what was out there, as surely as a caged wolf knows the face of his keeper. Near the top of the screen was a lichinous graygreen mass, looming through the bleakness, that he knew for a line of beaten, slumped mountains. Between the mountains and the dome was a plain, running with water, sodden with the runoff from the spineless hills, and in the water, the animals. They were the color of rocks at the bottom of an ocean—great, mud-plastered masses, wallowing toward each other in combat or in passion, rolling, lurching, their features gross, heavy, licking out a sudden paw with unbelievable speed, as though giant hippopotami, swollen beyond all seeming ability to move, still somehow had managed to endow themselves with the reflexes of cats. They crowded the plain, a carpet of obscenity, and for all they fed on each other, and mated, and sometimes slept with their unblinking eyes open and swiveling, they all faced toward the dome and never stopped throwing themselves against its flanks, there to hang scrabbling at the curve of the concrete, or doing more purposeful things.

Brendan looked out at them with his chest rising in deep swells. "I'd like to get out among you," he growled. "You'd kill me, but I'd like to get out among you." He took a long breath.

He triggered one of the dome's old batteries, and watched

the shells howl into the heaving plain. Red fire flared, and the earth trembled, erupting. Wherever the shells struck, the animals were hurled aside . . . to lie stunned, to shake themselves with the shock of the explosions, and to stagger to their feet again.

"You wait," Brendan hissed, stopping the useless fire. "You wait 'til my Donel gets at you. You wait."

He shut the screen off, and crossed his office toward a door set into the bulkhead at his right. Behind it were the nursery controls, and, beyond those, behind yet another door which he did not touch, was the quarter-portion of the dome that housed the children, sealed off, more massively walled than any other part, and, in the center of its share of the dome surface, pierced by the only full-sized gateway to the world. It was an autonomous shelter-within-a-shelter, and even its interior walls were fantastically thick in case the dome itself were broken.

The controls covered one wall of their cubicle. He ignored the shrouded camera screens and the locked switch that would activate the gate. He passed on to the monitoring instruments, and read off the temperature and pressure, the percentages of the atmospheric components, and all the other things that had to be maintained at levels lethal to him so that the children could be comfortable. He put the old headphones awkwardly to his ears and listened to the sounds he heard in the nursery.

He opened one of the traps in the dome wall, and almost instantly there was an animal in it. He closed the outer end of the trap, opened the access into the nursery, and let the animal in. Then, for a few more moments, he listened to the children as they killed and ate it.

Later, as he made his way down the corridor, going home for the night, he passed Chaim Weber's doorway. He stopped and listened, and coming through the foot-thick steel and the concrete wall, he heard the Channukah prayer:

"*Baruch Ata Adonai, Eloheynu Melech Haolam, shehichiyanu vikiyimanu, vihigianu lazman hazeh . . .*"

"Blessed be The Lord," Brendan repeated softly to himself,

"Our God, Lord of the universe. Who has given us life, and is our strength, and has brought us this day."

He stopped and whispered, "this day," again, and went on.

His wife was waiting for him, just inside the door, and he grunted a greeting to her while he carefully worked the bolts. She said nothing until he had turned around again, and he looked at her inquiringly.

"Sally?"

"You did it again," she said.

He nodded without special expression. "I did."

"Falconer's got the whole dome buzzing against you."

"All right."

She sighed angrily. "Did you have to threaten Lusic? He's only the representative of the previous generation. The one group inside the dome detached enough to be persuaded to back you up."

"One, I didn't threaten him. If he felt that way, it was only because he knew he was pushing me into a corner where I might turn dangerous. Two, anything he represents can't be worth much, if he can accuse me of bringing in a red herring and then can back down when I bring that selfsame herring back in a louder tone of voice. Three, it doesn't matter if anybody supports me. I'm in charge."

She set her mouth in a disgusted line. "You don't think much of yourself, do you?"

Brendan crossed the room. He sat down on the edge of the stone block that fitted into the join of floor and wall, and was his bed. Sitting that way, bent forward, with his shoulders against the curve of the overhead, he said, softly: "We've been married a long time, Sally. That can't be a fresh discovery you're making."

"It isn't."

"All right."

"You don't even care what *I* think of you, do you?"

"I care. I can't afford to pay any attention."

"You don't care. You don't care for one living soul besides yourself, and the only voice you'll listen to is that power-chant in your head. You married me because I was good breeding stock. You married me because, if you can't lead us outside, at least your son will be the biggest and best of his generation."

"Funny," Brendan said. "Lusic thinks I've been motivated by a fear of losing my pre-eminence. I wonder if your positions can be reconciled. And do you realize you're admitting I'm exactly what I say I am?"

She spat: "I hate you. I really do. I hope they pull you down before the nursery gate opens to the outside."

"If they pull me down, that'll be a sure bet. I changed over all the controls, several years ago. I'm the only man in this dome who can possibly work them."

"You *what*!"

"You heard me."

"They'll kill you when I tell them."

"You can think better than that, Sally. You're just saying something for the sake of making a belligerent noise. They don't dare kill me, and they'd be taking a very long chance in torturing me to a point where I'd tell them how the controls work. Longer than long, because there'd be no logic in my telling them and so passing my own death sentence. But I expected you to say something like that, because people do, when they're angry. That's why I never get angry. I've got a purpose in life. I'm going to see it attained. So you're not going to catch me in any mistakes."

"You're a monster."

"So I am. So are we all. Monsters with a purpose. And I'm the best monster of us all."

"They'll kill you the moment after you open that gate."

"No," he said slowly. "I don't think so. All the tension will be over then, and the kids will be doing their job."

"I'll kill you. I promise."

"I don't think you mean that. I think you're in love with me."

"You think I love you?"

"Yes, I do."

She looked at him uncertainly. "Why do I?"

"I don't know. Love takes odd forms, under pressure. But

it's still love. Though, of course, I don't know anything about it."

"You bastard, I hate you more than any man alive."

"You do."

"I—no . . . !" She began to cry. "Why do you have to be like this? Why can't you be what I want—what you can be?"

"I can't. Even though you love me." He sat in his dark corner, and his eyes brooded at her.

"And what do you feel?"

"I love you," he said. "What does that change?"

"Nothing," she said bitterly. "Absolutely nothing."

"All right, then."

She turned away in unbearable frustration, and her eyes rested on the dinner table, where the animal haunch waited. "Eat your supper."

He got up, washed at the sink, went over to the table and broke open the joint on the roast. He gave her half, and they began to eat.

"Do you know about the slaughtering detail?" he asked her.

"What about it?"

"Do you know that two days ago, one of the animals deliberately came into the trap in the dome? That it had help?"

"How?"

"Another animal purposely stayed in the doorway, to jam it. I think they thought that if they did that, the killing block couldn't fall. I think they watched outside—perhaps for months—and thought it out. And it might have worked, but the killing block was built to fall regardless, and it killed them both. The slaughtering detail dragged the other one in through the doorway before any more could reach them. But suppose there'd been a third one, waiting directly outside? They'd have killed four men. And suppose, next time, they try to wedge the block? And then chip through the sides of the trap, which are only a few feet thick? Or suppose they invent tools with handles, for leverage, and begin cutting through in earnest?"

"The children will be out there before that happens."

Brendan nodded. "Yes. But we're running it narrow. Very narrow. This place would never hold up through another generation."

"What difference does it make? We've beaten them. Generation by generation, we've changed to meet them, while all they've done is learn a little. We've bred back, and mutated, and trained. We've got a science of genetics, we've got controlled radioactivity, gene selection, chromosome manipulation—all they've got is hate."

"Yes. And listen to it."

Grinding through the dome, the gnaw and chip came to them clearly.

They began to eat again, after one long moment.

Then she asked: "Is Donel all right?"

He looked up sharply. They had had this out a long time ago. "He's all right as far as I know." He was responsible for all of the children in the nursery, not just one in particular. He could not afford to get into the habit of discussing one any more than another. He could not afford to get into the habit of discussing any of them at all.

"You don't care about *him*, either, do you?" she said. "Or have you got some complicated excuse for that, too?"

He shook his head. "It's not complicated." He listened to the sound coming through the dome.

She looked at him with tears brimming in her eyes. He thought for an instant of the tragedy inherent in the fact that they all of them knew how ugly they were—and that the tragedy did not exist, because somehow love did *not* know—and he was full of this thought when she said, like someone dying suddenly. "Why? Why, Sean?"

"Why?" She'd got a little way past his guard. "Because I'm the Captain, and because I'm the best, and there's no escaping the duty of being that. Because some things plainly must be done—not because there is anything sacred in plans made by people who are past, and gone, but because there is no other reason why we should have been born with the intelligence to discipline our emotions."

"How cut-and-dried you make it sound!"

"I told you it wasn't complicated. Only difficult."

The common rooms were in the center of the dome, full of relics: lighting systems designed for eyes different from theirs; ventilation ducts capped over, uncapped again, modified; furniture re-built times over; stuff that had once been stout enough to stand the wear of human use—too fragile to trust, now, against the unconscious brush of a hurried hip or the kick of a stumbling foot; doorways too narrow, aisles too cramped in the auditorium; everything not quite right.

Brendan called them there in the morning, and every man and woman in the dome came into the auditorium. They growled and talked restlessly—Falconer and Lusic and the rest were moving purposefully among them—and when Brendan came out on the stage, they rumbled in the red-lit gloom, the condensation mist swirling up about them. Brendan waited, his arms folded, until they were all there.

"Sit down," he said. He looked across the room, and saw Falconer and the others watching him carefully, gauging their moment. "Fools," Brendan muttered to himself. "If you were going to challenge me at all, you should have done it long ago." But they had let him cow them too long—they remembered how, as children, they had all been beaten by him—how he could rise to his feet with six or seven of them clinging to his back and arms, to pluck them off and throw them away from him. And how, for all their cleverness, they had never out-thought him. They had promised themselves this day—perhaps years ago, even then, they had planned his ripping-apart—but they had not dared to interfere with him until the dome's work was done. In spite of hate, and envy, and fear that turns to murder. They knew who their best man was, and Brendan could see that most of them still had that well in mind. He searched the faces of the people, and where Falconer should have been able to put pure rage, he saw caution lurking with it, like a divided counsel.

He was not surprised. He had expected that—if there had been no hesitation in any man he looked at, it would have been for the first time in his life. But he had never pressed them as hard as he meant to do this morning. He would need every bit of a cautious thought, every slow response that lived among these people, or everything would go smash, and he with it.

He turned his head fleetingly, and even that, he knew, was dangerous. But he had to see if Sally was still there, poised to one side of the stage, looking at him blankly. He turned back to the crowd.

"All right. Today's the day. The kids're going out as soon as I'm through here."

Sally had told him this morning not to call them together—to just go and do it. But they would have been out in the corridors, waiting. He would have had to brush by them. One touch—one contact of flesh to flesh, and one of them might have tried to prove the mortality he found in Sean Brendan.

"I want you in your homes. I want your doors shut. I want the corridor compartments closed tight." He looked at them, and in spite of the death he saw rising among them like a tide, he could not let it go at that. "I want you to do that," he said in a softer voice than any of them had ever heard from him. "Please."

It was the hint of weakness they needed. He knew that when he gave it to them.

"Sean!" Sally cried.

And the auditorium reverberated to the formless roar that drowned her voice with its cough. They came toward him with their hands high, baying, and Sally clapped her hands to her ears.

Brendan stood, wiped his hand over his eyes, turned, and jumped. He was across the stage in two springs, his toenails gashing the floor, and he spun Sally around with a hand that held its iron clutch on her arm. He swept a row of seats into the feet of the closest ones, and pushed Sally through the side door to the main corridor. He snatched up the welding gun he had left there, and slashed across door and frame with it, but they were barely started in their run toward his office before he heard the hasty weld snap open and the corridor boom with the sound of the rebounding door. Claws clicked and scratched on the floor behind him, and bodies thudded from the far wall, flung by momentum and the weight of the pack behind them. There would be trampled corpses in the auditorium, he knew, in the path between the door and the mob's main body.

Sally tugged at the locked door to the next section of corridor. Brendan turned and played the welder's flame in the distorted faces nearest him. Sally got the door open, and he threw her beyond it. They forced it shut again behind them, and this time his weld was more careful but that was broken, too, before they were through the next compartment, and now there would be people in the parallel corridors, racing to cut them off—racing, and howling. The animals outside must be hearing it . . . must be wondering . . .

He turned the two of them into a side corridor, and did not stop to use the welder. The mob might bypass an open door . . . and they would need to be able to get to their homes . . .

They were running along the dome's inside curve, now, in a section where the dome should have been braced—it hadn't been done—and he cursed Falconer for a spiteful ass while their feet scattered the slimy puddles and they tripped over the concrete forms that had been thrown down carelessly.

"All right," Brendan growled to himself and to Falconer, "all right, you'll think about that when the time comes."

They reached the corridor section that fronted on his office, and there were teeth and claws to meet them. Brendan hewed through the knot of people, and now it was too late to worry whether he killed them or not. Sally was running blood down her shoulder and back, and his own cheek has been ripped back by a throat-slash that missed. He swallowed gulps of his own blood, and spat it out as he worked toward his door, and with murder and mutilation he cleared the way for himself and the mother of his boy, until he had her safe inside, and the edge of the door sealed all around. Then he could stop, and see the terrible wound in Sally's side, and realize the bones of his leg were dripping and jagged as they thrust out through the flesh.

"Didn't I tell you?" he reproached her as he went to his knees beside her where she lay on the floor. "I told you to go straight here, instead of to the auditorium." He pressed his hands to her side, and sobbed at the thick well of her blood over his gnarled fingers with the tufts of sopping fur caught in their claws. "Damn you for loving me!"

She twitched her lips in a rueful smile, and shook her head slightly. "Go let Donel out," she whispered.

They were hammering on the office door. And there were cutting torches available, just as much as welders. He turned and made his way to the control cubicle, half-dragging himself. He pulled the lever that would open the gates, once the gate motors were started, and, pulling aside the panels on cabinets that should have had nothing to do with it, he went through the complicated series of switchings that diverted power from the dome pile into those motors.

The plain's mud had piled against the base of the gate, and the hinges were old. The motors strained to push it aside, and the dome thrummed with their effort. The lighting coils dimmed, and outside his office door, Brendan could hear a great sigh. He pulled the listening earphones to his skull, and heard the children shout. Then he smiled with his ruined mouth, and pulled himself back into his office, to the outside viewscreen, and turned it on. He got Sally and propped her up. "Look," he mumbled. "Look at our son."

There was blurred combat on the plain, and death on that morning, and no pity for the animals. He watched, and it was quicker than he could ever have imagined.

"Which one is Donel?" Sally whispered.

"I don't know," he said. "Not since the children almost killed me when they were four; you should have heard Donel shouting when he tore my respirator away by accident—he was playing with me, Sally—and saw me flop like a fish for air I could breathe, and saw my blood when another one touched my throat. I got away from them that time, but I never dared go back in after they searched out the camera lenses and smashed them. They *knew*, then—they knew we were in here, and they knew we didn't belong on their world."

And Falconer's kind would have gassed them, or simply re-mixed their air . . . they would have, after a while, no matter what . . . I know how many times I almost did . . .

There was a new sound echoing though the dome. "Now they don't need us to let them out, anymore." There was a quick, sharp, deep hammering from outside—mechanical, purposeful, tireless. "That . . . that may be Donel now."

AND THEN SHE FOUND HIM

THE SPECIAL MEETING of the Merchants' Protective Association was held on the second floor of the Caspar Building, above Teller's Emporium on Broad Street. Around seven o'clock, before anybody'd had a chance to more than half settle his supper, members began coming up the narrow stairs beside Teller's display window. Unsmiling, they sat down on folding chairs that lost their straight-rowed orderliness as small groups bunched together to talk in low, upset voices. In a short time the air was thick with cigar smoke, and the splintered old board floor was black with scuffled ashes. There was more than a touch of panic in the atmosphere.

Todd Deerbush sat alone and unnoticed in the back row, his bony ankles hooked over the crossbar of the seat in front of him. He looked tiredly out from under the brim of his khaki rainhat, and from time to time he pinched the bridge of his narrow nose. He and Stannard had rolled over four hundred miles today, and more than fourteen hundred in the past three days, to be in time for this meeting. Deerbush had driven all the way, while Stannard analyzed and re-analyzed the slim sheaf of newspaper clippings that had brought them here. Now Stannard was in a hotel room, sleeping. Tomorrow they'd rendezvous, Deerbush would give his report on this meeting, and the executive half of the team would begin work.

Deerbush was dog-tired. Because he could leave it to second nature, his mind worked on alertly, but his face fell into weary, unguarded lines. He was somewhere near forty, with features that could look either younger or much older. Most important were his eyes. They were set among radiating folds in his gray skin. Shadowed by pinched eyebrows, his eyes gave him the look of long-accustomed solitude—of a loneliness walled off and carefully, methodically sealed away.

In the front of the room, the chairman was calling the meeting to order. The minutes were approved as read and Old Business was tabled by acclamation. There was a dignified clinging to orderliness in the way the chairman ran faithfully through the parliamentary procedures. There was impatience in the nervous creak of the folding chairs. Men hunched forward, shuffled their feet, caught themselves and sat still, and then crouched again. Only Deerbush sat motionless, by himself in the back of the room.

"New Business?" the chairman asked, and immediately recognized a short, spare, balding man who'd gotten his hand in the air first. The man stood up quickly.

"I guess—" he began. "I suppose," he substituted self-consciously, "we all know why we're here. So there's no use talking about that. What we're here for tonight is to try and do something about it."

"If we can," another man broke in.

The first man waved a hand in sharp impatience. "If we can. O.K. But—what I was saying— We all know each other. I guess we've all checked with each other. It looks like my store's been hit the worst. Our inventory's short about a hundred dollars a week for the last two months."

Other men broke in now. The short man snapped: "Well, maybe my place isn't the worst. But, by golly, what's the difference in the end? Somebody's walkin' out with stuff from every one of our places, he's been doin' it for months, we're goin' crazy, and we can't even say how he's been doin' it.

And what's more, I guess there ain't a merchant here can stand that kind of stuff very long. 'Bout the only thing this feller ain't done yet is rob the bank—and maybe he's gettin' set to do that, too. The police ain't findin' anything out, the insurance detectives ain't no better, and neither's my store cop. If we don't do somethin' soon, this town—yessir, this *whole* town—is gonna be flat on its back and bankrupt! Now, what're we gonna do about it?"

Deerbush grunted to himself. He reached three fingers into the open package in his shirt pocket, took out a pinch of loose tobacco, and began chewing it thoughtfully.

Other men were standing up now. "All right, Henry. I'm going crazy over at my place, too. You say we ought to do something. But what? Things just disappear. In broad daylight. No one comes near them. Stock can't just float out the door—but one minute it's there and the next it isn't. I can't think of anything to do about that."

"An', by the way," another man put in, "I figure we'd be six weeks closer t'an answer if all you didn't keep shut t'each other about it that long. What's the good of this 'Sociation if we got t'read about these things in t'paper?"

"I didn't notice you standin' up and sayin' anythin', Sam Frazer," the spare man answered testily. "I don't mind admittin' I wasn't in a hurry to look foolish. Then I found out it wasn't just my place. But I guess after that I didn't try to make out I'm so smart, callin' down my fellow merchants in this community. You just sit down, Sam, and let the rest of us work this out. Before it gets to be more'n we can handle."

"We can't handle it now." The man who spoke hadn't said anything up to now. Deerbush had noticed him earlier hunched forward in the first row, a scorching cigarette held gingerly between his fingertips. He went on doggedly, in spite of his obvious embarrassment. "This isn't shoplifting as anyone has ever heard of it before. I've checked this with the men from my insurance company, and I've talked to Chief Christensen. I'm—I'm almost inclined to believe it's humanly impossible to be robbed in this particular way."

Deerbush fingered his nose again, and sat up straight. But

nothing was made of that half-idea, and the man who'd brought it up had nothing more to say.

It ended with the Association's deciding on offering a reward. It was a patently useless move, but it was something to put on the record. The meeting broke up lingeringly, with men snapping at each other and at nothing.

By then, Deerbush had a fair picture of things. More and more it became obvious that he'd been right in calling the newspaper stories to Stannard's attention.

The last man to leave the hall put the lights out and locked the door behind him. Deerbush stood up and shucked out of his trench-coat. Rolling it into a pillow, he took off his hat, stretched out on the floor, and went to sleep.

It was almost noon when he woke up. He got to his feet, ran his fingers through the thin, gray-brown hair left on his shiny scalp, and brushed off his suit with a few swipes of his palms. He looked out through the windows.

Outside, he saw Broad Street in the light of a brightly sunny day, with cars moving up and down the street and shoppers going into stores. But there were policemen on duty at every corner, and they neglected the traffic in favor of stealthily watching the people on the sidewalks. People-like, the shoppers evidently had not yet let a few stories in the weekly paper really sink in. But Deerbush could see one or two pedestrians looking at the police with sudden realization. It was a small town. Once started, it wouldn't be many days, or hours, before the panic he'd seen in this hall last night would osmose out from behind the store counters, puddle up, and begin to choke the whole town.

He settled his hat on his long, narrow skull, folded the trenchcoat over his arm and left the hall. He was thinking Stannard had better clean this up today if he could.

Stannard was waiting for him on the corner of Broad and Fauquier streets. They walked slowly along together, hugging the edge of the sidewalk, while Deerbush gave his report. Occasionally people bumped into them, and always moved on without apologizing. Whenever it happened, Stannard would grimace. Deerbush paid it no attention.

Stannard nodded slowly when the report was finished. "I think that confirms it," he said in his patient voice. "You agree, don't you, Todd?"

"We never had one of us turn out to be a criminal up to now," Deerbush answered, intending it to be no more than a comment.

Stannard turned to him patiently. "I'm surprised it hasn't happened before, Todd. You must remember the pressures and strains that arise in us from being as we are. Bear in mind that it's incredible that any of us, let alone most of us, grow up to be mature personalities."

"Sure, Frank. I didn't mean to say anything special by it. It's just that this kind of thing hasn't happened up to now."

"Of course, Todd. And I appreciate your getting help from someone else, instead of trying to handle it by yourself."

Deerbush shrugged uncomfortably. He knew very well that Stannard and the other people of his kind, back in Chicago, were all of them brainier than he was. The people at the top of the organization, like Stannard, were almost as much different from Deerbush as he was from most people. Maybe more. They seemed to live a different kind of life, inside—restless, tense; like people trying to climb out of a cage. Deerbush had thought about it for a long time, and decided it was because they could always spare a part of their brains for remembering the spot they were in.

He and Stannard walked along, and toward one o'clock they stopped at a diner next to the city hall. They finally got seats at the crowded counter after missing their turn twice, and then they waited a long time for the waitress to get their order. Stannard toyed with his fork. Deerbush was accustomed to this kind of thing, being among other people much more often: he called out their order as the waitress passed by, trusting to her training to leave it stuck in her mind. In time she came back along the counter, carrying two plates and looking up and down the row of customers.

"Hot roast beef and a ham on white?"

"Right here, Miss," Deerbush said in a deliberately loud,

firm voice. She set the plates down in front of them automatically, without looking at them. She was an attractive woman, near Deerbush's own age, with laughter lines at the corners of her mouth. Deerbush looked at her with almost naked hope in his eyes. But there was no disappointment in him when she turned away without ever having looked at the man behind this one of a row of faces.

Stannard looked at him, shaking his head. "Isn't your own kind good enough for you?" he said with gentle pointedness.

Deerbush shrugged uncomfortably. He ate quickly, left an oversized tip, went out, and waited for Stannard on the sidewalk.

They set a rendezvous, divided the town between them, and separated. Deerbush began walking along the streets south of Fauquier, turning casually into each store for a minute or two. Each time, he could smell the mute panic, thick as sour honey, clogging the air. Every place was the same; full of pale clerks who forced smiles at their customers and jerked their heads every time the door opened. But no one ever noticed him—no one stopped him to ask what he was doing. He moved along, stepping out of everyone's way, gathering urgency from the look of the people he saw.

Two o'clock found him walking quickly. By now he knew which stores had been hardest hit, and he thought he saw the pattern in the shoplifter's work. He wondered if Stannard mightn't have seen it some time ago, and possibly finished their job already. . . .

He walked into The Maryland Company—"The Complete Department Store"—and began moving back and forth along the aisles.

It was worse here than anywhere else in his half of town. The clerks were worked up to an edge of desperation that made them dig their pencil-points into their sales receipts and fumble at change-making until the customers caught the infection too. No one talked in a normal tone of voice.

He saw how many people there were who stood motionless and went over everybody with their eyes, and that told him how frightened the insurance companies were. And there was a stock-taking crew, moving hurriedly from counter to counter, making spot-checks—not quite at random.

They'd seen the pattern, too. Deerbush nodded to himself at the efficiency of the system, even though it couldn't ever catch this special thief.

He went to the Misses' Dress Department. There were more tensely idle people concentrated around it than anywhere else in the store. Deerbush stopped, leaned against a pillar, and waited, ignored. And eventually, almost at closing time, he saw her.

She walked into the department with a number of packages already under her arm; a tall, pale, thinnish woman. Her brown eyes were large, her nose was short and upturned. Her lips were pursed in a cupid's bow. Her hair was short and black, carefully dressed, with just the faintest dusting of silver at the tips. She moved lightly—not gracefully, as grace is taught, but with quick, unsettled movements that reminded Deerbush of a small young bird. Her gown was pale pink and summery, with bows at the shoulders and a ruffle of thick petticoats at the hem. Except for the deep creases in her forehead and the sharp definition of her lips, it might have been easy to mistake her age.

Her glance swept the dress racks and adjoining accessory counters. She looked at handbags, her lower lip caught between her teeth, and shook her head. She pivoted on one heel. The detectives all looked past her, preoccupied.

Deerbush was sure.

He watched her approach the dress racks and begin lifting things out. After a moment, she went over to the saleswoman, who was picking nervously at a floss of lint on her skirt.

"Hello," she said softly.

The saleswoman came to life. Her face lit a warm smile that was all the more strange for the abstracted look in her eyes. Deerbush grunted explosively.

"Why, hello there, miss!" she beamed fondly. "My that's a pretty frock!" And still, there was something vague in her expression.

The girl dimpled. "Why, thank you!" she smiled. And the

detectives continued to ignore her, just as they ignored Deerbush.

Now the girl twined her fingers behind her back and bowed her head, blushing. "But you have so many other pretty ones here," she whispered shyly.

"Why, bless you, dear, do you mean you'd like to have some of them?" The saleswoman looked contrite for not having thought of it sooner. But Deerbush could see something trapped in the saleswoman's eyes. Something that knew there was a wrong thing going on, but couldn't get its knowledge through.

"Oh! Could I?" the girl in the summery dress exclaimed, clapping her hands together. "They're so beautiful!"

"Of course dear," the saleswoman soothed. "Here—come with me—here's where the really nice ones are. You just pick out the ones you like."

Deerbush watched wonderingly. The girl lifted dress after dress off the racks, holding each against herself and turning in front of the big floor-length mirrors. She never looked directly at her own face—only at the dresses. Deerbush had the feeling she was too self-conscious to be caught admiring herself.

Finally, she and the saleswoman had chosen a group of dresses.

"Thank you *very* much!" the girl breathed.

"I'm glad you like them, my dear," the saleswoman said, smiling warmly. "Please come back again." And still there was something lost and trapped in her expression, but it was very faint.

The detectives stayed watchful, but all of them seemed to have found something—a curled edge in the carpeting, or a turning overhead fan—that kept attracting their attention.

"I'll come back," the girl said. "I promise." She turned to go, holding the dresses. "Goodbye!"

"Goodbye, dear," the salesgirl said. She smiled fondly, if vaguely, and drifted back behind her counter. She looked down at her skirt, began scraping harshly at the fabric.

The girl in the summery dress moved slowly toward the doors, browsing as she went, stopping at an occasional counter to look over the merchandise. Once she waited while a floorwalker stepped abstractedly out of her way.

Deerbush moved after her. He heard a sound behind him and felt it raise the hackles of his neck. He spun his head around. The stock-taking crew was in the Misses' Dress Department and the saleswoman was doubled over her counter, sobbing hysterically. "No—no," she was saying, "there wasn't anybody here."

A man held the front doors open for the girl in the summery dress. Deerbush was on the street only yards behind her, brushing by the store detective who unobtrusively blocked the exit. He followed her as she turned off the main street away from the shopping areas, and he couldn't make sense out of what he'd seen.

But that didn't matter so much—the important thing was that he'd found her.

He could tell she'd never had anyone follow her before in her life. She never looked about her. When she turned off into a tree-lined side street, Deerbush stepped up beside her.

He walked there for perhaps twenty steps before she turned her head and looked at him, frowning a little. She peered at him with puzzled eyes. "You're different," she said.

"It's all right," Deerbush said, trying not to frighten her. "My name's Todd Deerbush and I'm not going to hurt you. I'd like to walk along with you for a while."

She stopped still. "You're different," she repeated. "You're like me."

Maybe, Deerbush thought. "I don't know," he said.

She began walking again, finally, the dresses forgotten in her arms, puzzling over it. "You noticed me," she said after a while, her mind made up. "All by yourself. Nobody else ever did. You must be real too."

"I don't know what you mean by that," Deerbush said gently. "But people don't notice me, either."

She nodded firmly. "Unless you make them. You're real . . . I never thought anybody else but me was real."

"I guess there's quite a few," Deerbush answered, thinking that there were none exactly like her. "But it's hard to tell.

Might be some in every town. Far's I know, I'm with the only bunch that's gotten together."

"Are there that many of us?"

"Well," he said, "there's more than fifty in this bunch I'm in."

They walked a little farther. They were in a very good neighborhood now, with big houses and wide lawns. She turned toward him again, and looking at her he realized she'd been preoccupied all the while. "What makes us real, Todd?"

He still didn't know what she might mean by that. He tried to answer her as best he could. "Stannard—that's one of our real smart people; you better ask him for the answers—Stannard says we broadcast—like a TV station, he says—something like that; it's out of my league—that makes us not be noticed. It works inside people's heads." He felt he was making himself sound confused and stupid. He couldn't help it, and he was used to it.

"That's not what I asked you, Todd. That's what happens first. But after a while you can make people notice you and be nice to you. But they can't do it to you. That proves you're real and they're just . . . something else. But what *does* it?"

"The same kind of thing, I guess," he answered lamely. He was trying to find out more from her than she could from him, and he didn't know what to do about it. Stannard might—but for some reason Deerbush found himself not wanting Stannard in this right now. "Stannard says it's protection. He says Mother Nature's working out a new kind of creature in us, and doesn't want us to get hurt. But she kind of overdid it."

His voice was gentle. He thought of her growing up in this town, with the broadcast growing stronger and stronger as she grew; wondering why the boys didn't have any interest in her, wondering why everyone acted so strange. He could see the puzzled little child with the tear-streaked face, and the hurt teen-ager who came later, having to separate from her family if she was to live at all . . . and then the woman, blooming somehow in spite of everything, and beginning to fade . . . Only she'd found something.

A warm and exciting thing was happening to Deerbush.

He felt he was really coming to understand her. He'd been no different, before he had the idea of setting himself up in this kind of work. Twenty years of living a settled life had let him strike a balance with himself and get along with what he was. But when he looked at the girl; thin, pale, worn and terribly lonesome, he could understand how it would be for her.

Except that it wasn't the same, he reminded himself. She had something else.

But, looking at her, he couldn't see it. He could only see, under her eyes, the hollows that makeup couldn't quite take out.

"Where're you from, Todd?"

"Chicago, now."

"I've always wanted to see places like that. I suppose I could." She touched her upper teeth to her lower lip. "But I *knew* I was real as long as I stayed here."

They reached a trimmed hedge with a white picket gate set in the middle of it, and a walk going up to a white house with window boxes and ruffled white curtains in the windows.

"My name is Viola Andrews," she said. "I live here. Would you like to come inside and visit with me?"

She showed him through the house. The living room was full of beautifully carved, heavy walnut furniture, with overstuffed divans and easy chairs. There were standing lamps with beautifully decorated shades, and delicate end-tables with china figurines on them. The kitchen had an electric mixer, a toaster, a rotisserie, an electric frying pan, a dishwasher, big refrigerator, and freezer.

As she showed him from room to room, she held his arm. Her grip grew tighter, and her voice more excited. "I can't get over it, Todd. Someone else like me! Aren't these chairs pretty? I had some others, but then I saw these, and I had them sent over right away. I've done that with most of my furnishings—there are so *many* nice things in the stores. But tell me some more about yourself, Todd, please. I'm dying to know all about you. How were you when you were a little boy? Was it as terrible for you as it was for me?"

"I don't know, Vi." He felt more and more awkward as she

clung to his arm and led him from room to room. Her bedroom had gilded antique furniture, with delicate French dolls propped up on satin pillows over the pink bedspread. The dining room had cupboards full of fragile china and sculptured silver cutlery.

"Isn't it all beautiful? Oh, Todd, I'm getting more and more excited by the minute! I can't get *over* you!'

Suddenly she stopped. Her fingers dug into his arm. "It was awful, Todd," she said intently. "After I left my parents, I still tried so hard to be like other girls. I had to . . . not pay . . . for my food all of the time, but I tried in everything else. And then, one day not long ago, I was twenty-five." She touched an embroidered handkerchief to the corners of her eyes. "I suddenly realized I was going to be alone forever, for as long as I lived. Other girls were married, they had families, they had all the things a girl needs—and I was never, never going to have them. It was like a deep black closet with myself crouched in the very far corner, and no way out.

"I—I didn't know what to do. I had to make *somebody* notice me. I was ready to die if somebody didn't. And—and—" her voice suddenly rose, "and one day, I *could*! I didn't know how, but I just *could*! I didn't have to be a thief any longer. I didn't just have to get along on as little as I could. I could make people like me, and pay attention to me, and give me presents."

Just as suddenly, she bowed her head. "But they're just pretending, and I know it," she whispered. "They're not real. They don't really see me or like me. They forget me just as soon as I go away."

She straightened and took her hand from his arm. She touched an embroidered handkerchief to the corners of her eyes. "I'm so glad you came to help me that I can't even put it into words; but I am glad, Todd."

Deerbush shook his head. He'd been pretty badly worried when he first read the newspaper stories. But it wasn't that one of his own kind of people had turned out bad, which was what he'd been afraid of at first. It was just this girl, scared, trying to fill in what she'd been missing. He put his arm around her shoulders.

"Listen, Vi," he said, "best thing to do's get you out of here as quick as we can, and get you with your own kind of people."

"Thank you, Todd," she said in her breathless voice. "You're very nice to me." She hugged him impulsively.

"Listen—" he said, trying to think of how to tell her what he wanted to. "Vi—see, what I am, is a marriage broker."

"A marriage broker?"

"Uh—yes—see, what it says I am in the Chicago Classified is a private investigator. People never see me. They just call up the AA Agency on the phone, and I mail 'em reports on the people they want to find out about. That's how I make my living. But what I really do, for this bunch of our people, is go around the country looking for more. And when I find one, I try and fit them to somebody else that hasn't got a husband or wife. It's a thing I figured out to do, so I could be somebody useful."

That had been the easy part. Now he was stopped again.

He wished he was smarter, so he could know what was wrong with Vi. He knew there was something wrong, something that somebody like Stannard could put his finger on in a minute. But he knew too that it didn't matter. Underneath it, she wasn't bad, or vicious. She didn't do these things because she was mean. She was gentle, and hurt, and lost. If a man had time, he could bring out the good things in her. A man who understood her, and took care of her, and was patient with her, could do it.

"Vi—what I mean is, I've found plenty of women for other men. I liked a lot of them—I'm not trying to fool you about that—but I never . . . What I mean is, these women all had a lot on the ball. And the other men in this bunch're a lot more deserving. They sort of belonged together, and I knew it." He stopped to listen to what he'd said, and went red. "I don't mean," he blurted, "you don't stack up to 'em. I don't mean that at all, Vi. You're a lot smarter than me, and I know it. I'm not much. But what I mean is, I've always taken these women back to Chicago with a man in mind for them. But—" He reached out for her hands. "Not this time." He didn't sound like himself.

"Vi—I'm not much, and I don't have much. I do work that's bound to keep me away from home a lot, and with people like us that's going to be extra hard on you, but—"

"Oh, Todd," she said, coloring, "I'm the happiest girl in the world!"

He couldn't believe it. He stood looking at her, holding her hands, and for a long moment he couldn't get it through his head. Then he felt warmth all through him, and he had to close his eyes for a minute because he was smiling as hard as she was.

"We better get going as soon as we can," he said, "try and get a start while it's still daylight. We've still got to pick up Stannard, and my car. So I'll ask you to pack fast. Better just take one suitcase."

She pulled sharply away from him. "One suitcase? You mean—leave all my nice things?"

He'd known it couldn't last. "Well—sure, Vi. They don't belong to you . . ."

She stamped her foot in anger. "Leave all my *presents*? I won't! I won't do it!"

"Vi," he said patiently, "you've got to."

"No!"

"Look, Vi, feeling that way doesn't make sense. You took that stuff. Somebody's stuck for the money somewhere. But it's not just that. You've got this town scared; you've got it scared so bad these people're going to stampede and hurt themselves. They're ready for it—it's plain as day, all over town. You want something like that on your conscience?

"If you leave the stuff here, that'll take care of it. They'll find it after a while, and they'll decide it was a smart crook. It'll be a puzzle for them, but it won't be building up anymore. They'll have their stuff back and after a while they'll forget about it—if it never happens anywhere again.

"And even if you don't think they're real anyhow—the stuff still doesn't belong to you. You didn't earn it."

"You're awful!" she shouted at him. "You're mean and

awful. I don't like you at all. You hate me. Get out of here!"

"Vi——"

"I hate you! I hate you!" She pulled her hands back awkwardly and hit him with the heels of her fists. "I won't give up my nice presents! I won't! I like getting presents—I want lots of nice things to have! I want lots of nice things—I want a lot more than I have! And I don't *like* you! Get away from me! Go away! Go away!"

Deerbush sighed. "All right, Vi."

"I'm going to go downtown and get more nice things—lots more. And don't you try and stop me!"

"I'm sorry, Vi," he said in a voice that had no life in it, "but it looks like I better come back in a hurry."

Walking quickly toward his rendezvous with Stannard, he saw police cars cruising the streets. The men inside them drove slowly, their heads turning as they looked at every pedestrian except Deerbush. He noticed they were paying special attention to the women, and he wasn't too surprised. But they'd never find her. They might come and knock on her door, and maybe even talk to her, but they'd never find her. It would just get worse and worse.

He wondered how bad it could get. After the first stores had to close—or if Vi began going into people's houses—what would these people living here in this town do? Would they be wearing guns here in this town, looking back over their shoulders all the time, locking everything up? And still losing things? And if it came to the militia and martial law, or the state police or F.B.I., and they still lost things—what then?

A car up the street jammed on its brakes. The doors flew open, and the detectives inside jumped out on the sidewalk. They ran up to a startled plump woman and surrounded her. One of them flashed a badge for an instant. The others had already grabbed the packages out of her arms and were tearing them open. The woman looked from one to another of them, her face white, her mouth twisted by shock.

There was nothing Deerbush could do to help her. He stood

watching it, cursing in a voice so low he didn't hear it. But he couldn't help feeling a little jolt of relief as he thought nothing like that could ever happen to Viola.

"I wish I'd found her," Stannard sighed as they drove toward Viola's house.

"I shouldn't have said I wanted her to come to Chicago." Deerbush said. What hadn't worked out between him and Vi was a personal thing, and a private hurt, but what he'd done was make trouble for everybody.

"You couldn't know that, Todd," Stannard was telling him. "You had no way of guessing. She was something brand new to you—brand new to anyone, for that matter, in this variation. You're quite right—they'd never find her. Between the curiosity-damping field, and this new ability that seems to spring directly from her arrested emotional development, it's —well, it's more than fortunate that I came here with you." He stared out at the dark street for a moment. "It's a horrible shame she's so completely crippled, has so little moral stamina in her makeup. But what an ability! Intelligently, maturely used—you realize, don't you, Todd, that this could easily be the answer to the problem of the damping field? I'm afraid she's past hope, but if we could learn it from her . . . Well, that makes no difference. We can always raise her children apart from her, so they'll have her heredity but not her hysteria."

"I guess we could," Deerbush said.

"She didn't tell you what it is she does?"

Deerbush shook his head. "Sounded like she doesn't know, herself. She just does it. People—people give her presents."

"She simply wishes people would obey her, and that's all? She walked up to this saleswoman, you say, and caused the woman to give her the dresses."

"I know. But the woman *wanted* to."

"And had hysterics afterward, claiming she knew nothing about it. Well, that part's the damping field, taking hold again after whatever else it was had done its work. Would you describe to me, again, this expression you say you saw on the clerk's face? It sounds to me as though there might be something valuable in that . . ."

They were in front of Viola's house. "No lights," Deerbush said, feeling almost glad. "She's gone. We'll have to look for her." Now Stannard would have to keep quiet, and leave him alone.

Stannard was peering at the dark house. "Do you think she'll come back here? We have to find her quickly. I want her in Chicago as fast as we can bring her, and I want her isolated from human beings before she has half the world giving her things and the other half howling for her blood."

"We'll find her. We just have to go down along the shopping street." *I wish I was the richest man in the world,* he thought.

They drove back toward the main street, both of them quiet. They passed a police car, its spotlight fingering the sidewalks.

"The stores aren't open late tonight," Stannard said.

"I don't think that's going to make any difference." They turned onto the main street. It lay empty but guarded, most of the storefronts lit by night lights, the parking spaces bare along the curbs except for places where occasional men—insurance detectives, Deerbush guessed—sat in plain cars reading newspapers. Foot patrolmen walked silently from door to door, each with only one block for his beat, trying locks. A radio car rolled up the street to the intersection that marked the end of the double row of stores, made a U turn, came down to the intersection of Broad Street and Riverside Avenue, made another U turn, and rolled up the street again.

At the corner of Broad and Fauquier, where The Milady Shop was located, Viola stood waiting while a middle-aged man fumbled at the shop door with his keys.

"Is that she?" Stannard asked.

Deerbush nodded. "That's her." He eased the car to a stop at the curb.

"I'll talk to her," Stannard whispered.

Viola was intent on the man opening the shop door, but she turned her head as Deerbush and Stannard hurriedly crossed the sidewalk toward her.

The shopkeeper was paying neither of them any attention.

He had the door open now, and he spoke to Viola. "There you are, little honey. Now, I told you it wouldn't take but a minute or two, didn't I?"

Viola took an indecisive step toward the door. Her face was clouded up angrily, and when they were close, she said in a low, angry voice, "You get away from me, you!"

Stannard whispered to Deerbush: "My God, she's acting like a five-year-old!"

Deerbush thought of how sensitive and delicate she was, and how helpless she'd be without this extra something she could do.

"Something wrong, little honey?" the shopkeeper asked Viola, his voice full of concern.

"Make them go away!" Viola cried, stamping her foot.

"Make who go away, little honey?"

"Can't you see them? You see them. See them and make them go away!"

"Miss Andrews—" Stannard began.

Deerbush was looking at the shopkeeper. He had never seen anyone try so hard to do something that ought to be so easy. He and Stannard weren't invisible. But the shopkeeper advanced uncertainly, brushing his hands in front of him like a man going into a long hall full of cobwebs. Then his fingertips touched Stannard. For just a second, he almost did the impossible because Viola had asked him to. His eyes looked into Stannard's face and Deerbush could see them almost begin to focus. But then the shopkeeper's head lolled forward on his chest and he stumbled back against his window. He leaned on the glass, his lips slack, looking at nothing. His breathing became shallow and monotonous.

"I hate you!" Viola spat at him. "You don't like me!"

"Miss Andrews—" Stannard said again. He was pale as he looked at the shopkeeper.

Viola pointed at Deerbush. "*You* help me." she said to Stannard. "Make him leave me alone!"

A foot patrolman passed by them, turned to the door of the next shop, tested the lock, and went on.

Stannard was motionless, staring at her.

Then Stannard said to her: "Don't worry, dear—everything's fine. Everything's all right. I'll take care of you. You don't have to worry." His voice was soothing, and only someone who knew Stannard as well as Deerbush did could have noticed the peculiar note it struck, as if somewhere, too deep in his throat to win the fight, something was trying to choke off the words.

He turned suddenly and tried to hit Deerbush.

"Oh, thank you!" Viola exclaimed. "You're nice. You'll get rid of the nasty man for me."

Deerbush felt the blow on his shoulder. He tried to get a hand on Vi's arm before she could run away, but he couldn't with Stannard between them. He elbowed Stannard back, but he had to drop his shoulder to do it. Stannard swung again, and this time he split Deerbush's cheek.

Deerbush shook his head sharply.

"Get away from her," Stannard panted. "Stop bothering her!" Viola took two quick steps forward and pushed her hands against Deerbush's chest.

"You stay away from my presents," she mumbled angrily.

"I'm sorry, Frank," Deerbush said. He stepped back, holding one of Vi's wrists now, and with the other hand he hit Stannard hard on the jaw. As Stannard fell down, Vi began to scream.

Deerbush held her wrists for a long moment while she kicked and kicked at his legs. He looked at Stannard, lying on the sidewalk, and saw the man's eyes start to flutter open.

He let go of Vi's wrists and reached with his hands, drawing up his shoulders and lowering his face to protect it from her fingernails. "I'm sorry, Vi."

Deerbush waited until the police car had rolled by. Then he pulled his old sedan away from the curb, and pointed the car toward the edge of town, driving with both hands on the wheel and only vaguely feeling the hurt places in the skin of his face.

Stannard was sitting hunched in the seat beside him. He rubbed his jaw. "It was incredible," he mumbled. "I never for a moment considered that she might be able to use her ability on one of us."

"All right," Deerbush said.

"I'll never forget it. I knew what she was. I didn't change my judgment of her by one iota before she spoke to me. And then, suddenly, she was the most wonderful person in the world. She deserved everything anyone could offer her. It was right that she be made happy. It was *unthinkable* that anything should be permitted to interfere with her wishes. I would have laid down my life for her."

"All right, Stannard," Deerbush said. He was blinking, and searching the sides of the road with his eyes. He wished Stannard would be still.

"No—no, it's not all right." Stannard shook his head. "Can you imagine what would have happened? If she could make me obey her, she could make any of us obey her. God! Suppose we'd succeeded in getting her to Chicago! Fifty of us, all her slaves. You never could have stopped it. We'd all have been against you." Stannard twisted around to stare fascinated into the back seat, where Deerbush had gently laid Vi down, "You were right to do that, Todd. You were never more right in anything in your life."

Deerbush was more tired than he had ever been. He felt haunted, and he knew that that was something he would never lose.

He saw the church beside the road, its spire and walls a flat bulking shape in the darkness, solid only where the edge of his headlight beam touched the weathered brown shingles. He stopped the car and got out. He opened the trunk and then walked over to the rusted pipe railing that ran around the churchyard. He stood there for a little while, and then he went back to the opened trunk of the car. He came around to Stannard carrying a hubcap he'd pried loose with the big screwdriver from the tool box, and the flat steel top of the box itself.

"Here," he said. "We can use these to dig with."

Stannard got unsteadily out of the car. "She was like a petulant child," he said. "It was love she demanded. Absolute, complete love."

Deerbush thrust the hubcap into his hands. "Here," he said. "We'd better get this done. And quit harping on it."

"Yes," Stannard said vaguely. "Of course. Deerbush—what could stave off a demand like that? *Why* couldn't she get to you?"

Deerbush leaned over into the back seat and lifted Vi out, holding her with all the gentleness he had. He cradled her in his arms.

"All her life she looked for it—" he said, "for just one person who could *really* love her. . . . And then she found him."

THE SKIRMISHER

It was a hot day, and near noon, when Ben Hoyt pulled the unmarked radio car to a stop in front of the house. He cut the motor and ran his hand around his neck, where the starch in his collar was leaving a red weal like a rope burn. He thought: One of these days I'm going to marry a woman just to quit using those damned laundries.

But he hadn't been thinking about starch. Not really; it had just been the sound his brain made, idling, while he listened to the steady, monotonous rhythm of rifle shots coming from behind the house. They were sharp and spiteful, and they echoed flatly through the palmetto scrub and turpentine pine behind the house. Hoyt got out of the car and unbuttoned his suit coat so he could get at the .45 stuck in his waistband. Then he closed the car door quietly and walked toward the back of the house. The shots kept up in driving succession, one after the other in a group of three, then a pause, then another group of three.

The house was a new ranch type, with light green stuccoed walls and a low tile roof, with a close-cropped lawn and a solar hot water heater up on the south face of the roof. It was set in a good-sized lot, about four hundred feet to a side, and had a waist-high cinder block fence that walled off the front and sides of the lot, running back into a stretch of pine barren that just kept going until it merged into the Everglades. It looked odd all the way out here, as if a man had wanted to keep inconspicuous and still didn't want to get cheated out of living as if he were in a town.

Hoyt came around to the back of the house with his hand on his .45 just for luck, but he'd had it figured right. The man lying on the ground, squinting through the backsight of a rifle, was shooting at a row of paper targets set at distances of fifty, a hundred, and a hundred and fifty feet away from him. The rifle he was using looked like a standard .22, but it was making too much noise and recoiling much too hard. It had to be a rechambered wildcat model, kicking a .22 slug out of a shell case necked down from a 30-30, or maybe even something heavier.

The man on the ground was about thirty. He was sunburned and as hard as something carved out of solid mahogany. He was wearing a pair of ragged shorts made out of an old pair of denims, and nothing else. There were full and empty boxes of shells lying scattered on the ground all around him. There were fired shell cases strewn out like a glittering carpet to his right. A half-full glass of liquor with the ice almost melted was set down in easy reach. He had a cigarette hanging out of the left side of his mouth, and there were ashes all up and down his sweaty left arm. Hoyt watched. The man pumped a shot into the fifty-foot target, the hundred, and the hundred and fifty, flicking the backsight up a notch every time he palmed the bolt and fed another round into the chamber. His shoulder jumped every time he fired, and the ashes shook off the end of his cigarette. Hoyt looked out past the targets, and every shot was tearing holes in a log backstop. There were white chips of wood trailed out behind it for a good twenty feet.

"Four-oh-eight," the man on the ground muttered to himself. "Four-oh-nine, four-ten."

"Hey, there," Hoyt said.

The man on the ground grimaced and looked back over his shoulder. He had close-cropped black hair, flattened on top, a flat, small face with close-set eyes, heavy ears, and a thin nose that had been knocked over to one side. "Yeah?" Other than that, he didn't move.

Hoyt held out his badge. "You Albert Madigan?"

"That's right."

"My name's Hoyt. Wade County Sheriff's office. Want to talk to you."

Madigan shrugged. "Well, go ahead." He flipped the back-sight down and fired into the fifty-foot target. "Four-eleven." The target was cut to ribbons in a scattered group that ranged from around the ten ring to absolute bogeys. The other two targets were even worse. Madigan moved his sight and squeezed off a shot into the hundred-foot target. It punched out wide at four o'clock. "Four-twelve."

"Hey there, I said I wanted to talk to you. Haven't got all day."

Madigan dropped the clip out of the rifle and fed in a new one from a pile of them he had lying on the ground under his chin. "Well, squat down and talk. I'm not about to go anywhere." He put a shot in each of the targets. "Four-fifteen," he muttered, turning on his side and massaging his right shoulder. There was a purplish-red blotch on his skin.

"Stand up, punk," Hoyt said with his fist on the butt of the .45.

"Go chase ducks," Madigan said. He rolled back over on his stomach and the rifle barked three times. "Four-sixteen, four-seventeen, four-eighteen," he muttered.

Hoyt pulled his .45 out and pointed it at the back of Madigan's head. "Stand up, I said."

Madigan looked back over his shoulder. "Go ahead and shut me, Bud. Do you a whole lot of good."

Hoyt stood over him cursing, with the sweat going down the back of his shirt.

Madigan grinned up at him. "Or is there something you want to find out from me?"

Hoyt took a stubborn breath. "Four years ago, a man named Stevens went off the Overseas Highway into the Gulf. His car busted through the guard rail and the barracuda got him. A little later, a man named Powers was getting off the *Champion* at Boca Raton when his foot slipped. He went under the wheels, and the train was still rolling. He was a damn fool for jumping the stop, but he'd of made it if he hadn't put a foot in a busted hair tonic bottle. The bottle wasn't there a minute earlier. Somebody dropped it ahead of him. And Stevens drove into a sheet of newspaper that was blown out of the car in front of him."

"Tough," Madigan said. "Tough, and out of the county, too. What's your beef?"

"Three years ago, a woman named Cummings jumped off Venetian Causeway into the bay. *That's* in the county. And last year a kid named Peterson was riding a motor scooter up U. S. 1 when his back tire blew. He went across the road in front of a trailer truck, and that was in this county, too. After that, there was a fellow named Pines. Diabetic. Went to a drugstore, got some insulin. Came in a sealed box of little glass bottles. Took it home, snapped the neck off one of the bottles, filled his hypo, gave himself a shot. It wasn't insulin. Somebody'd gotten the boxes mixed up in the drugstore refrigerator. After that, there was a man named—"

"Make your point."

"All right. The Cummings woman jumped because her boyfriend called her up and told her he was going back to Oklahoma with his wife. Only the boyfriend never called her. Fellow in a lunch counter phone box heard this other fellow in the next booth. Didn't take much notice of it until after she made the papers. Then he told us about this fellow: Five eight or nine, broken nose, black hair, half-moon scar on his right cheek. The boyfriend didn't look one bit like that. How good're you at imitating voices, Madigan?"

Madigan grinned. The scar on his cheek lost itself in the wrinkles.

"We didn't have much to tie that on to. We let it ride. The boyfriend wasn't even married. Now, this Peterson kid on the scooter. He hit a piece of board with a nail on it. The board fell off a truck in front of him. There was a fellow sitting on the tail-gate. Hitch-hiker. The driver remembers him because he wanted a ride up to Dania, and after the accident when he got there he crossed the road and started to thumb back toward Miami. Looked like you."

"Lots of people look like me," Madigan said, grinning like a reptile.

"Quit stalling around, Madigan," Hoyt said, hefting the .45 in his hand. "I got a busy schedule."

Madigan shrugged. "Tough."

Hoyt narrowed his eyes. Madigan had a funny, dangerous look about him. Hoyt had seen a few men like him during the last war—guys who'd got caught in combat, somewhere, and whipsawed to the point where they knew they were going to die. Then, for some reason, they got out of it, but after that they didn't care about anything. Nothing could touch them any more, and they were very hard to kill. Still, it took a lot of combat to get a man to a point like that, and Hoyt wondered just where somebody Madigan's age could have found enough of it. "You want to see me get tough, Madigan?"

Madigan shrugged. "Suit yourself, Bud. Seeing you're so busy, though, why don't you come back when you can say what you want me for?"

"I know what I want you for," Hoyt said coldly. "How long did you think you could get away with it?"

"With what?"

"Come off it, Madigan. We tied you up with the Cummings woman. We tied you up with the Peterson kid. We know you delivered that mislabeled phony insulin. The same kind of car as the one you rented that day was barrelling down the road in front of the Stevens car when it went into the Gulf. So us, and the Howard County cops, and the state cops, we got together and started comparing notes. See, we had this funny coincidence to work with: that diabetic was going to get married the next day, and the Peterson kid was on his way up to

Allandale to run off and elope with this high school freshman. And one of the Howard County cops remembered these other three cases in the past two years, where people got accidentally killed just before they were going to get married. So he checked it, and what do you know?—there was this same guy, with the same funny scar, mixed up in all three of them somewhere."

"Yeah?" Madigan was smirking.

"Yeah! So we started taking it from the other end. We went into the marriage license records, and checked out everybody in south Florida who took out a license but never got married. And, you know what? Fifty-three of them died. Fifty-three in five years. Now, you figure it out. That's a lot of accidents. So we checked 'em. Some of them turned out to be for real. Some of them, we're not so sure. But guess who else we found on the list? Two people: Powers, the guy on the train, and Stevens, the guy in the car. What's the matter, Madigan—you hate newlyweds, or something?"

Madigan grinned and shook his head. "I don't give a damn for newlyweds one way or the other. It's their grandchildren that bother me."

"Make sense," Hoyt growled.

"Nah—nah, *you* make sense. You tell me how the county prosecutor's going to convince a jury that anybody in the Year of Our Lord 1958—"

"'57," Hoyt corrected automatically.

"Okay, '57." Madigan shrugged. He looked at Hoyt like somebody on the right side of the bars in a zoo. "You just tell a jury how a man could rig those accidents."

"We'll figure it out."

"You couldn't do it in seventy-four years, Bud. And that's a fact. Well, so long, Hoyt."

Madigan turned suddenly and started to run, but he wasn't trying hard. He loped easily, barefoot, picking his steps with care.

"Stop!" Hoyt shouted.

Madigan grinned back over his hard shoulder and kept loping, dodging perfunctorily toward a tree now and then.

"Stop!"

Madigan kept running. Hoyt raised his heavy .45 and shouted for the last time: "Stop!" He fired over Madigan's head.

The heavy recoil jarred his arm. He took a small step to correct his balance, and his foot nudged the half-full glass of liquor over on its side. His foot slipped in the mess of suddenly wet shell cases, and he fought wildly to keep from falling. The .45 flew out of his hand, and Madigan was out of the handgun's short range. Hoyt scooped up the abandoned rifle, thumbed the sight, and fed a round into the chamber. He put the head of the hooded foresight between Madigan's shoulder blades and squeezed the trigger. And the weakened chamber burst, exploding jagged steel into his skull.

He lay in the pine needles and shell cases, blind and relaxed. He heard Madigan stop running and come walking casually back, but that was no longer any affair of his.

It was a comfortable feeling, knowing you were going to die in a minute, before the shock could possibly wear off and let the waiting pain reach you. It freed you of the problem of your messed-up face. It freed you of any problem you cared to name.

There, now—it was beginning to hurt just a little. Time to go, Hoyt—time to go . . . slip down, slip away . . . that waitress at the lunch counter . . . hell, Hoyt, you've got the best excuse in the world for not keeping that date with her tonight. . . .

THE MAN WHO TASTED ASHES

THE CAR HE'D stolen was a beautifully groomed thing: all polished lacquer and chrome, with almost brand-new dual tread whitewall tires on the nickeled wire wheels. But the transmission was bad, the brake drums scraped, and there was a short circuit in the wiring somewhere, so that he had to keep over sixty miles per hour or the generator would not charge at all. He would have stolen another one if he could, but he had got onto the turnpike before he realized just how unreliable this one was. If he changed cars at a restaurant, it would be reported and the police would stop him when he tried to leave the turnpike.

No, he was trapped with what he had. Hunched over the wheel of his roaring cage, the yellowish headlights reflecting white from the lane markers, Redfern swept his eyes systematically over the instruments: ammeter, fuel gauge, oil pressure, water temperature, speedometer, odometer. He thought of himself as doing it systematically, every ten minutes, like a professionally trained driver. Actually, he was dividing his attention almost equally between the road and the odometer. A hundred and ten miles covered, seventy miles to go, ninety minutes before the ship was due to take off, with or without him, average speed required: 42.62, approx.; round off to allow for stopping the car at the exit toll booth, for covering two miles of back roads, for leaving the car and running an unknown distance across a weed-grown field to the ship's airlock—they would take off on schedule with him six inches from the slamming airlock door; they would not stay themselves a microsecond to accommodate him—say fifty miles per hour, average. Then allow for speedometer error. Say fifty-five miles per hour, indicated, average. Allow for odometer error. Say sixty miles per hour, indicated, average. Allow for unforeseen delays. Sixty-five miles per hour.

Redfern's foot trembled on the accelerator pedal. His thigh ached from hours of unremitting pressure. His car flashed by signboards, wove continually around immense trailer trucks in the slow lane. His mind raced to keep up with the changing figures on the odometer. He wished he weren't feeling a slight miss in the engine whenever he eased up on the accelerator. He cursed the car's owner for his false-front prodigality with wax and whitewalls.

He looked at his watch again. Four in the morning. He

turned the radio on, ignoring his fear that something else might happen to the car's wiring.

"—And that's the news," the announcer's professionally relaxed voice said. "After a word about United Airlines, we'll hear, first, Carl Orff's *Carmina Burana*, followed by—"

His watch was slow.

Five minutes? Fifteen minutes? How long did the news take?

He held the watch to his ear. It was an expensive one, wafer thin, beautifully crafted, left over from his younger days—he could barely hear it running. Was it running at all?

Redfern was a leathery man, his yellowish-white hair brushed back from angular temples, a scruffy Guards moustache over his nearly invisible lips. His suits were made for him by a London tailor, from measurements taken in 1925; they were gored and belted in the backs of the jackets. Outdoors, he wore a Burberry and carried a brief-case. People who saw him on the street in Washington always took him for someone with diplomatic connections. But since Redfern was always seen afoot, these connections perforce had to be minor. Was he an assistant attaché of sorts, perhaps? At his age? Looking at Redfern, people would wonder about it.

People. But the man who'd sat easily on the edge of Redfern's lumpy bed in the wallpapered hotel room—that man, now . . .

That man had coal-black hair, broad, flat cheekbones above a sharply narrowing chin, oval, maroon-pupiled eyes and cyanotic lips. He smiled easily and agreeable across the room.

Redfern sat in the one chair, sipping at the water tumbler half-full of gin. The bottle his visitor had brought up was standing on the bureau. His visitor, who had given the name of Charlie Spence, was not drinking.

"You don't look like a Charlie," Redfern said abruptly over the tumbler's rim. "You look as cold as ice."

Spence laughed, his small mouth stretching as far as it could. "Maybe I'm made of it," he said. "But then, you're

C*

nothing but a lump of coal. Carbon." He brushed his fingertips together.

"But then," Redfern mocked sharply, "*I* don't pretend to be gregarious."

"Oh, I don't pretend—don't pretend at all. I *am* gregarious. I love the company of people. I've been moving about among them for several years, now."

"All right," Redfern said sharply, "we've already settled that. Let's let it be. I don't care where you come from—I don't really care what you're made of. It may surprise you, but I've thought for some time that if people were coming to this world from other places, they'd be bound to get in touch with me sooner or later."

"Why on Earth should we try to get in touch with you?" Spence asked, nonplused.

"Because if you people have been coming here for years, then you're not here openly. You've got purposes of your own. People with purposes of their own generally come to me."

Charlie Spence began to chuckle. "I like you," he laughed. "I really do. You're a rare type."

"Yes," said Redfern, "and now let's get down to business." He gestured toward the bureau top. "Pour me some more of that." Alcohol affected him swiftly but not deeply. Once it had stripped him of the ordinary inhibitions, he could go on drinking for some time before his intellect lost its edge. Since he always took two aspirins and went straight to bed at that point, it was not a serious sort of weakness. But without his inhibitions he was a very unpleasant man.

"It's a simple business," Charlie Spence was saying a little later. "The ambassador will land at National Airport and be met by the usual sort of reception committee. Red carpet, band, dignitaries, and so forth. But the red carpet will be a little shabby, the band won't be first-rate, and the reception committee will not be quite as high-ranking as it might be. After all, the ambassador's country is definitely on the other side of the fence."

"Yes," Redfern drawled. "The protocol of prejudice."

"Oh, no, no, nothing deliberate," Spence said, with a hand raised. "Diplomats pride themselves on equal courtesy to all. But the employee in charge of caring for the carpets simply won't do his best. The band won't play with any great enthusiasm. And any of your officials who happen to be ill, with colds or similar afflictions, will honestly decide their health precludes the effort of attending. This is simply human nature, and any snub will be completely unintended."

"I heard you the first time. What's all this to do with me?"

"Well, now," Charlie Spence explained, "the ambassador's not from a particularly large nation in their bloc. It seems doubtful they'd bother to send along any of their own security police. The only guards present will likely be American Secret Service personnel, extending courtesy protection."

"Yes."

"So. In the first place, the ambassador is really a small fish. In the second place, no American, even a trained professional sworn to his duty, is apt to be quite as devoted to the ambassador's life as he would be to that of, say, any American congressman. Those two factors represent a potential assassin's margin of safety."

"And what're you meddling in our politics for?" Redfern growled.

"*Your* politics? Redfern, my dear fellow, it may or may not be your planet, but it's most assuredly our solar system."

The neck of the bottle tinked against the lip of Redfern's glass. "And I'm your assassin?"

"You are."

"What makes you think I'll do it?" Redfern cocked his head and looked narrowly at Spence.

"A compulsive need to meddle in human history."

"Oh?"

Charlie Spence laughed. "You were cashiered from your country's foreign service in nineteen hundred and thirty-two. But you've never stopped mixing into international situations. Gun running, courier work, a little export-import, a little field work for foreign development corporations . . . and, now and then, a few more serious escapades. Don't tell me you don't enjoy it, Redfern. It's a very hard life, all told. No one would stay in it as long as you have if it didn't satisfy his need for power."

Redfern pinched his lips together even more tightly, in the fleeting reflex with which he always acknowledged the truth. "I wasn't cashiered," he said. "I resigned without prejudice."

"Oh, yes; yes, you did. Being unpleasant to one's superiors doesn't disgrace a man—it merely makes him unemployable. Except for special purposes that don't require a pukka sahib. And here I am, as you said, with a special purpose. Ten thousand dollars, on completion, Redfern, and the satisfaction of having started World War III."

Redfern's eyes glittered. "All over one little ambassador?" he asked carefully.

"Over one little ambassador. In life, he's not considered worth the trouble of protecting him. And no one but a rather stout and liverish woman in the Balkans will mourn him in death. But when he dies, his side will suddenly discover a great and genuine moral indignation. Why? Because they will be truly shocked at such a thing happening in America."

"World War III," Redfern said ruminatively.

"Exactly. You'll shake the ambassador's hand. An hour later, when he's already safe inside his embassy refreshing himself after his trip, he'll fall into a sudden coma. The embassy will close its doors, issue a misleading statement, and call its doctor."

"Yes."

"Very well. The embassy staff has taken routine steps, and waits for the ambassador to recover. But, just to allow for all eventualities, the unofficial courier service is already transmitting a notification to the government at home. The doctor examines the patient and discovers an inflamed puncture on his right hand. Another message goes home. The ambassador dies, and tests indicate poison. Obviously, it was hoped the puncture would go unnoticed and the cause of death, which resembles cerebral occlusion, would be mistaken. But the tiny needle must not have been quite sterilized, by accident, and the clever doctor has penetrated the scheme—and another message goes home, before the American State Department even suspects anything serious."

"Hmm. I'll simply shake his hand?"

Charlie Spence reached into his pocket. "Wearing this." He held out a cumpled something, the size of a handkerchief. Redfern took it and unfolded it. "A mask," Spence said. "Drawn over your head, it will mold new features for you. It'll be devilish uncomfortable, but you won't have to wear it long."

"It'll make me look like someone entitled to be on the field?"

Spence grinned the grin of a Renaissance Florentine. "Better than that. It will give you the composite features of six people entitled to be on the field. You will look like none of them, but you will look superficially familiar to anyone who knows any of them. The subsequent questioning of witnesses will yield amusing results, I think."

"Very clever. Good technique. Confuse and obscure. But then, you've practiced it a long time." Redfern pushed himself abruptly out of the chair and went into the adjoining bathroom, keeping the door open. "Excuse me," he said perfunctorily.

"Lord, you're a type!" Charlie Spence said. "Will you do it?"

"What?" Redfern said from the bathroom.

"Will you do it?" Spence repeated, raising his voice.

Redfern came out, picking up the gin bottle, and sat back down in the chair. He tipped the bottle over the glass. "Maybe."

"I've told you too much for you to back out now," Spence said with a frown.

"Rubbish!" Redfern spat. "Don't try to bully me. You don't care what any of the natives tell each other about you. There are dozens of people living off their tales about you. It's to your advantage to hire native helpers wherever you can —if they're caught, who cares what wild tales they tell? You'd be insane to risk losing one of your own people." He looked sharply into Charlie Spence's eyes. "I don't suppose you fancy the thought of a dissecting table."

Charlie Spence licked his lip with a flicker of his tongue. "Don't be too sure of yourself," he said after a moment, in a more careful tone of voice.

Redfern snorted. "If I acted only on what I was sure of, I'd still be an embassy clerk."

"And you wouldn't like that, I suppose?" Charlie Spence, recovered, was looking around the room. "Sometimes? At night, when you can't sleep?"

"I want an out," Redfern said brusquely. "I won't do it without accident insurance."

"Oh?" Charlie Spence's eyebrows quivered.

"If I'm caught in the field, I'm caught and that's it. I'll protect you."

"Professionalism. I like that. Go on—what if you get away from the field?"

"If I get away, but there's trouble, I want a rendezvous with one of your ships."

"Oh, ho!" Charlie Spence said. "You do, do you?"

"I'll cover my tracks, if you think it's important, but I want a rendezvous. I want to be off this planet if there's trouble. Change that—I want to be off it in any case, and if there's no trouble, I can always be brought back."

"Oh, ho!" Charlie Spence repeated with a grin. "Yes, I'd think you *would* want to watch the next war from some safe place." It was easy to see he'd been expecting Redfern to lead up to this all along.

"Have it your way," Redfern said ungraciously.

Charlie Spence was laughing silently, his eyes a-slit. "All right, Redfern," he said indulgently. He reached into his card case, took out a photograph of a dumpy blonde woman and a string-haired man on the porch of a middle western farmhouse, and carefully split it with his thumbnails. Out of the center, he took a bit of tissue paper, and stuck the front and back of the photograph together again. Replacing the card case in his pocket, he handed the slip of paper to Redfern.

"Dip it in your drink," he said.

He watched while Redfern complied, but kept his eyes away from the short handwritten directions the alcohol brought up.

"Don't repeat the location aloud. I don't know it, and don't want to. Memorize it and destroy it. And I tell you now, Redfern, if the ambassador doesn't die, there'll be no ship." He smiled. "For that matter, you have no guarantee there'll be any ship at all."

Redfern growled. "I know."

"Lord, what meager hopes you live on, Redfern!"

"You're through here now, aren't you?" Redfern said.

"Yes . . ." Charlie Spence said with pursed lips.

"Then get out." He took the palm hypodermic Charlie Spence handed him in its green pasteboard box, and closed the hotel room door behind his visitor.

Thirty-five miles to go. His watch now read 4:30. It hadn't stopped, but was merely slow. If he'd thought to have it cleaned by a jeweler, last year or even the year before that, it would be accurate now. As it was, he had less than an hour, and he would be off the turnpike fairly soon, onto roads that were paved but had been laid out in the days of horse-drawn wagons.

He tried another station on the radio, but that was playing popular music. A third was conducting some sort of discussion program about water fluoridation. And that was all. The rest of the dial yielded only hisses or garbled snatches from Minneapolis or Cincinnati. His ammeter showed a steady discharge as long as the radio was on, no matter how fast he drove. He turned it off and steered the car, his face like a graven image. He was seething with anger, but none of it showed. As an adolescent, he had made the mistake of equating self-possession with maturity, and had studiously practiced the mannerism, with the inevitable result that he had only learned to hide his feelings from himself. He was the prisoner of his practice now, to the extent that he often had to search deep to find what emotion might be driving him at any particular time. Often he found it only in retrospect, when it was too late.

That lunch with Dick Farleagh this afternoon . . .

It had been difficult even to reach him: a call to the embassy—"*Who* shall I tell Mr. Farleagh is calling? Mr. Redfern?" and then the barely muffled aside, a whispered "Oh, dear." Then the pause, and finally, with a sigh: "Mr. Farleagh will speak to you now, Mr. Redfern," as though the secretary thought a bad mistake was being made.

"Dickie," Redfern said heavily.

"What is it, Ralph?" Farleagh's voice was too neutral. Obviously, he had taken the call only out of curiosity, because he had not heard directly from Redfern in nearly fifteen years. But he must already be regretting it—probably he didn't like being called Dickie, now that his junior clerk days were well behind him. Redfern ought to have thought of that, but he was in a hurry, and hurry, like liquor, always took away his social graces.

"I have to speak to you."

"Yes?"

Redfern waited. Only after a moment did he understand that Farleagh had no intention of meeting him in person.

"I can't do it over the telephone."

"I see." Now the voice was crisp, as Farleagh decided he could meet the situation with routine procedure. "I'll ask my secretary to make an appointment. She'll call you. Can you leave a number?"

"No, no, no!" Redfern was shouting into the telephone. "I won't be fobbed off like that!" His words and actions were registering on his consciousness in only the haziest way. He had no idea he was shouting. "This is too important for your blasted conventionalities! I won't put up with it! I have to see you." His voice was wheedling, now, though he did not realize that, either. "Today. No later than lunch."

Farleagh said with quiet shock, "There's no need to rave at me. Now, take hold of yourself, Ralph, and perhaps we can talk this out sensibly."

"Will you come or won't you?" Redfern demanded. "I'll be at the Grosvenor bar in an hour. I'm warning you you'll regret it if you don't come."

There was a long pause, during which there was a sudden

buzz in the phone, and the sound of Redfern's coin being collected. In a moment, the operator would be asking for another dime.

"Are you there?" Farleagh asked with maddening detachment. "See here, Redfern—" now the tenor of his thinking was unmistakeable in his voice, even before he continued—"if it's a matter of a few dollars or so, I can arrange it, I suppose. I'll mail you a check. You needn't bother to return it."

"Deposit ten cents for the next three minutes, please," the operator said at that moment.

"I don't want your blasted money!" Redfern cried. "I have to see you. Will you be there?"

"I—" Farleagh had begun when the operator cut them off.

Redfern stared in bafflement at the telephone. Then he thrust it back on its cradle and walked briskly out of the booth.

He waited in the Grosvenor bar for an hour and a half, rationing his drinks out of a sense that he ought to keep his head. He was not a stupid man. He knew that he always got into quarrels whenever he'd been drinking.

He rationed his drinks, but after the first one he did so out of a spiteful feeling that he ought to, to please that stuffed shirt Farleagh. He already knew that if Farleagh appeared at all, their meeting would not do the slightest good. Hunched over his drink, glowering at the door, he now only wanted to be able to say, afterwards, that he had made the utmost effort to do the right thing.

Farleagh came, at last, looking a great deal beefier than he had when he and Redfern were in public school together. His handshake was perfunctory—his maddeningly level gray eyes catalogued the changes in Redfern's face with obvious disapproval—and he practically shepherded Redfern to the farthest and darkest table. Obviously, he did not relish being seen in a public place with a man of Redfern's character. Redfern drawled: "You've gone to fat."

Farleagh's eyes remained steady. "And you to lean. What is it you want, Redfern?"

"If it isn't money?" Redfern's mouth curled. He turned and signaled to a waiter. "What will you have, Dickie?"

"None for me, thank you," Farleagh said in an impassive drone. "I'm pressed for time."

"Are you? You've no idea, do you, that I might be on a close schedule myself." Redfern glanced at his watch. The ambassador's plane was due at National Airport in two hours, and there was a great deal still to be done. "You've kept me waiting." He waved the waiter away in sudden irritation, without ordering. "Now, you listen to me," he told Farleagh. "I'm going to be at a definite place and time tonight. Here." He flicked the balled bit of tissue paper across the table into Farleagh's lap.

Farleagh picked it out and transferred it to a side pocket. He would have been a very bad diplomat if he had ignored it. But it was plain he was merely providing for an extremely remote possibility. "Redfern," he said, "if you're attempting to involve my government in some scheme of yours, that will be the end. You'll have gone too far."

"*Our* government, Dickie," Redfern almost snarled. "I still carry my passport."

"Precisely," Farleagh said. "I'm sure the American authorities would deport you, at our request. If you stand trial at home, you'll not get off easily."

"There's nothing in my past record that breaks the law at home."

"There's a great deal about you that breaks laws more popular than those in books."

"Damn you, Farleagh," Redfern said in a voice he did not know was high and almost tearful, "you'd better be there tonight."

"Why?"

"Because if you aren't, and I do get involved in something, it'll be found out soon enough that you could have been there. I warn you now, Farleagh, if I go down, it won't be easily. Perhaps it won't matter to *you* if *your* career's smashed. I tell you now, there's a great deal more involved in this than your career."

Farleagh was still not taking his eyes away from Redfern's face, nor moderating the set of his mouth. He gave the appearance, sitting there in his expensive suit, with his graying black hair combed down sleekly, of enormous patience nearly at an end.

"Very well, then!" Redfern exclaimed. "I don't care if you believe me or not." He thrust his chair back. "But if someone gets ill who shouldn't, today, you'd better believe me!" He stalked away, his Burberry flapping from his arm, his brief-case banging into the backs of chairs, his face an unhealthy red.

He drove vengefully, in a rage that included the car and the radio, his watch, Farleagh, Charlie Spence and the world.

Five o'clock, by his watch. He turned into the exit ramp with a squealing from the tires, and one part of his mind was hoping there would be a blowout, just to prove something to the car's owner. He touched the brakes almost reluctantly, and at the same time cursed their criminal softness. He fumbled on the seat beside him for the toll ticket, and searched in his nearly empty wallet. He had had to spend a good deal of money today—more than he'd expected, for the drug and the explosive. It had never been his intention to steal a car, but rental had been out of the question. He knew, and damned the fact, that another man might have gotten better prices with his suppliers. But what sort of logic was there in making up to criminals; slapping their backs and buying them drinks, talking to them on an equal basis, when he could not even see the need to do that sort of thing in his dealings with respectable people?

He slapped the ticket and his two remaining dollar bills into the toll attendant's palm, and accelerated again without bothering even to look toward the man. He had seen no sign of drawn-up police cars anywhere around the toll plaza. That was the important thing, the only important thing at the moment.

Now that he was off the turnpike, he forgot he had been so afraid of being stopped for automobile theft. It had been another in a succession of thin-edged risks which could be shown to extend back to the beginning of his independent life. He forgot it as he had forgotten his fears concerning all the others—as he had forgotten that he had been afraid something would go wrong at the airport this afternoon, or that he would be caught as he hung about in Washington for hours afterward, until he was sure the embassy was acting as if something were wrong behind its doors.

As he drove now, forcing his car around the twisting mountain corners, he had other things to be afraid of.

Farleagh might not be there—might have been stubborn, or unaccountably stupid, or simply too slow, in spite of the margin Redfern had allowed him. He looked at his watch again as he turned off onto a dirt track leading almost straight up the hill. Five-twenty by his watch. He had perhaps five minutes.

He took one deep breath—one, and no more, just as he had done at the airport gate this afternoon, and as he had done on other occasions in his life—and drove the car into a tangle of shrubbery just past a mortared-stone culvert that was his position marker. He shut off the ignition and sat as if stupefied by the engine's silence. Almost instantly, the headlights were no more than a sickly orange glow upon the leaves pressed against the car's grille. He shut them off, picked up his briefcase, and abandoned the car. Burberry flapping around his thighs, he trotted across the road and plunged down a slight decline into a stand of tamaracks. It was dark except for the remaining light of a low half-moon seeping through the overcast.

He moved with practiced efficiency through the trees, keeping his direction by paralleling the brook that had trickled through the culvert, until he emerged without warning into an open and long-neglected field, choked with proliferating brush, entirely surrounded by evergreens, with the spaceship, tall as an oil refinery's cracking tower, standing in its center.

The airlock door in the side of it was open. Redfern began to force his way through the brush, toward the extended ladder which connected the airlock with the ground. There was a single light in the lock chamber. No other lights were visible—the ship was a complex silhouette of struts and vanes, given the reality of depth only by that open door, and what that door might lead to, Redfern could not really guess.

As he struggled up to the ladder, he was arming the satchel charge in his briefcase.

There was still no sign of life from inside the ship. But as he climbed the ladder, hoisting himself awkwardly with his one free hand, the ladder began to retract with the sound of metal sliding into metal, and other mechanical sounds resonated out of the hull, like generators coming up to speed, and relays in a sequence of switching operations. He looked up and saw the airlock door quiver and begin to turn on its massive hinges.

With a strained motion of his arm, he threw the charge overarm into the airlock, and let go the ladder. He heard the briefcase thump to the deck in the lock chamber, while he himself was falling ten or twelve feet back to the ground. When the explosion came, he was sprawled on the ground, rearing up on his out-thrust arms, and he stared in fascination at the flame-shot billow of orange smoke gouting through the still half-open lock.

He rolled, off to one side, as the outer door rebounded from the hull. He was afraid it might fall on him, but then he saw it was still hanging, like a broken gate.

The starting-noises inside the ship came to a complete stop. He had done what he had hoped to do—breached the hull, and activated the safety cut-offs in the controls. The ship was caught, earthbound, possibly not for very long, but perhaps for long enough.

The brush crackled and plucked at his passage. He could not bring himself to look away from the ship, and he blundered through the undergrowth with his arms behind him, feeling his way. The light in the airlock chamber was off now, but something was still burning in there, with a dull smoldering red flicker.

A hand placed itself flat between his shoulderblades. "All right, easy now, sir," a voice said.

He turned convulsively, his face contorted as if by pain, and made out a tall, huskily built young man in a narrow-brimmed hat, who was holding a short-barreled revolver in his other hand. The brush was parting all around him—there were many men here—and suddenly a portable floodlight shot up a beam to strike the airlock.

"We were just about ready to send a man aboard when you crippled them, sir," the young man said with his trained politeness.

"Is Farleagh here?" Redfern demanded.

"Yes, sir, Mr. Farleagh's back among the trees, with the chief."

A man had stepped up to the base of the ship, where the ladder had rested. Like Redfern's young man, he wore a civilian suit as if it had been made by a uniform manufacturer. "Aboard the ship!" he shouted up through cupped hands. "Can you hear me? Do you speak English? This is the Secret Service."

There was a grating sound up in the lock chamber, as someone forced open the balky inner door. Then a man stumbled up to the edge and looked down, his white coveralls smudged and a strained look on his face. He squinted at the Secret Service man.

"Jesus Christ, yes, I speak English," he said in outrage. "Who threw that bomb? This is a goddam Air Force project, and there's gonna be all kinds of hell."

"Oh, no, you don't!" Redfern shouted, mortally afraid things could still go wrong. "It won't wash—not with me to testify against you."

The Secret Service man at the base of the ship turned his head in Redfern's direction long enough to show his exasperation. Then he pointed his pistol up at the man in the lock. "Jump down, you."

There was the sound of someone heavy coming toward them through the brush. After a moment, Farleagh said: "There you are."

"Hullo, Dickie." Redfern grinned at Farleagh in the spottily reflected light. "Now you know."

"Know what?" Farleagh asked heavily.

Redfern shifted his feet nervously. "Why I got myself cashiered years ago. You see I knew they were coming here—at least, I believed they were—and I decided what sort of human being they would be mostly likely to contact."

Rage crossed Farleagh's face at last, and shocked Redfern. "Stop it, Redfern," he said savagely. "For once in your life, admit you're the sort of man you are."

After that, no one seemed to look at him. An improvised ladder was brought up, and Secret Service men went into the ship and came down again escorting sullen, blue-lipped men.

LOWER THAN ANGELS

THIS WAS ALMOST the end. Fred Imbry, standing tiredly at the jungle's edge, released the anchoring field. Streaming rain immediately began coming down on the parked sub-ship on the beach. The circle of sand formerly included in the field now began to splotch, and the sea dashed a wave against the landing jacks. The frothing water ran up the beach and curled around Imbry's ankles. In a moment, the sand was as wet as though nothing had ever held that bit of seashore free.

The wind was still at storm force. Under the boiling gray sky, the craft shivered from half-buried landing jacks to needle-nosed prow. Soggy fronds plastered themselves against the hull with sharp, liquid, slaps.

Imbry trudged across the sand, slopping through the water, wiping rain out of his face. He opened the sub-ship's air-lock hatch, and stopped, turning for one look back into the jungle.

His exhausted eyes were sunk deep into his face. He peered woodenly into the jungle's surging undergrowth. But there was no sign of anyone's having followed him; they'd let him go. Turning back, he hoisted himself aboard the ship and shut the hatch behind him. He opened the inside hatch and went through, leaving wet, sandy footprints across the deck.

He lay down in his piloting couch and began methodically checking off the board. When it showed green all around, he energized his starting engines, waited a bit, and moved his power switch to *Atmospheric.*

The earsplitting shriek of the jet throats beat back the crash of the sea and the keening of the wind. The jungle trees jerked away from the explosion of billowing air, and even the sea recoiled. The ship danced, off the ground, and the landing jacks thumped up into their recesses. The sand poured out a shroud of towering steam.

The throttles advanced, and Imbry ascended into Heaven on a pillar of fire.

CHAPTER I

Almost at the beginning, a week earlier, Fred Imbry had been sitting in the *Sainte Marie's* briefing room for the first time in his life, having been aboard the mother ship a little less than two weeks. He sat there staring up at Lindenhoff, whose reputation had long ago made him one of Imbry's heroes, and hated the carefully schooled way the Assignment Officer could create the impression of a judgment and capacity he didn't have.

Around Imbry, the other contact crewmen were listening carefully, taking notes on their thigh pads as Lindenhoff's pointer rapped the schematic diagram of the solar system they'd just moved into. Part of Imbry's hatred was directed at them, too. Incompetents and cowards though most of them were, they still knew Lindenhoff for what he was. They'd all served under him for a long time. They'd all been exposed to his dramatics. They joked about them. But now they were sitting and listening for all the world as if Lindenhoff was what he pretended to be—the fearless, resourceful leader in command of the vast, idealistic enterprise that was embodied in the *Sainte Marie.* But then, the mother ship, too, and the corporation that owned her, were just as rotten at the core.

Lindenhoff was a bear of a man. He was dressed in iron-gray coveralls; squat, thick, powerful-looking, he moved back and forth on the raised platform under the schematic. With the harsh overhead lighting, his close-cropped skull looked almost bald; naked and strong, a turret set on the short, seamed pillar of his neck. A thick white scar began over his right eye, crushed down through the thick jut of his brow ridge, the mashed arch of his blunt nose, and ended on the staved-in cheekbone under his left eye. Except for the scar, his face was burned brown and leathery, and even his lips were only a different shade of brown. The bright gold color of his eyebrows and the yellow straw of his lashes came close to glowing in contrast.

His voice was pitched deep. He talked in short, rumbled sentences. His thick arm jerked sharply each time he moved the pointer.

"Coogan, you're going into IV. You've studied the aerial surveys. No animal life. No vegetation. All naked rock where it isn't water. Take Petrick with you and do a mineralogical survey. You've got a week. If you hit anything promising, I'll extend your schedule. Don't go drawing any weapons. No more'n it takes to keep you happy, anyhow. Jusek's going to need 'em on VII."

Imbry's mouth twitched in disgust. The lighting. The platform on which Lindenhoff was shambling back and forth, never stumbling even when he stepped back without looking behind him. The dimensions of that platform must be clearly imprinted in his mind. Every step was planned, ever gesture practiced. The sunburn, laid down by a battery of lamps. The careful tailoring of the coveralls to make that ursine body look taller.

Coogan and Petrick. The coward and the secret drunkard. Petrick had left a partner to die on a plague world. Coogan had shot his way out of a screaming herd of reptiles on his third contact mission—and had never gone completely unarmed, anywhere, in the ten years since.

The rest of them were no better. Ogin had certified a planet worthless. A year later, a small scavenger company had found a fortune in wolfram not six miles away from his old campsite. Lindenhoff hadn't seen fit to fire him. Kenton, the foul-minded pathological liar. Maguire, who hated everything that walked or flew or crept, who ripped without pity at every world he contacted, and whose round face, with its boyish smile, was always broadcast along with a blushingly modest interview whenever the *Sainte Marie's* latest job of opening up a new solar system was covered by the news programs.

Most of those programs, Imbry'd found out in the short time he'd been aboard, were bought and paid for by the Sainte Marie Development Corporation's public relations branch.

His thin hands burled up into tight knots.

The mother ships and the men who worked out of them were the legends of this generation—with the *Sainte Marie* foremost among them. Constantly working outward, putting system after system inside the known universe, they were the bright hungry wave of mankind reaching out to gather in the stars. The men were the towering figures marching into the wilderness—the men who die unprotestingly in the thousand traps laid by the unknown darkness beyond the Edge; the men who beat their way through the jungles of the night, leaving broad roads behind them for civilization to follow.

He had come aboard this ship like a man fulfilling a dream—and found Coogan sitting in the crew lounge.

"Imbry, huh? Pull up a chair. My name's Coogan." He was whipcord lean; a wiry, broadmouthed man with a tough, easy grin and live brown eyes. "TSN man?"

Imbry'd shaken his hand before he sat down. It felt a little unreal, actually meeting a man he'd heard so much about, and having him act as friendly as this.

"That's right," Imbry said, trying to sound as casual as he could under the circumstances. Except for Lindenhoff and possibly Maguire, Coogan was the man he most admired. "My enlistment finally ran out last week. I was a rescue specialist."

Coogan nodded. "We get some good boys that way." He

grinned and chuckled. "So Old Smiley slipped you a trial contract and here you are, huh?"

"Old Smiley?"

"Personnel manager. Glad hand, looks sincere, got distinguished white hair."

"Oh, Mr. Redstone."

Coogan grinned. "Sure, Mr. Redstone. Well—think you'll like it here?"

Imbry nodded. "It looks like it," he said carefully. He realized he had to keep his enthusiasm ruthlessly under control, or else appear to be completely callow and juvenile. Even before he'd known what he'd do after he got out, he'd been counting the days until his TSN enlistment expired. Having the Corporation offer him a contract on the day of his discharge had been a tremendous unexpected bonus. If he'd been sixteen instead of twenty-six, he would have said it was the greatest thing that could have happened to him. Being twenty-six, he said, "I figure it's a good deal."

Coogan winked at him. "You're not just kiddin', friend. We're on our way out to a system that looks pretty promising. Old *Sainte Marie's* in a position to declare another dividend if it pays off." He rubbed his thumb and forefinger together. "And how I do enjoy those dividends! Do a good job, lad. Do a bang-up job. Baby needs new shoes."

"I don't follow you."

"Hell, Buddy, I got half of my pay sunk into company stock. So do the rest of these guys. Couple years more, and I can get off this goddam barge and find me a steady woman, settle down, and just cash checks every quarter for the rest of my life. And laugh like a sonavabitch every time I heard about you birds goin' out to earn me some more."

Imbry hadn't known what to make of it, at first. He'd mumbled an answer of some kind. But, listening to the other men talking—Petrick, with the alcohol puffing out on his breath; Kenton, making grandiose plans; Maguire, sneering coldly; Jusek, singlemindedly sharpening his bush knife—he'd gradually realized Coogan wasn't an exception in this crew of depraved, vicious fakes. Listening to them talk about the

Corporation itself, he'd realized, too, that the "pioneers of civilization" line was something reserved for the bought-and-paid-for write-ups only. He wasn't dewy-eyed. He didn't expect the Corporation to be in business for its health. But neither had he expected it to be totally cynical and grasping, completely indifferent to whether anyone ever settled the areas it skimmed of their first fruits.

He learned, in a shatteringly short time, just what the contact crew men thought of each other, of the Corporation, and of humanity. They carped at, gossiped about, and despised each other. They took the Corporation's stock as part of their pay, and exploited all the more ruthlessly for it. They jockeyed for favored assignments, brought back as "souvenirs" anything valuable and sufficiently portable on the worlds they visited, and cordially hated the crews of all the rival mother ships. They weren't pioneers—they were looters, squabbling among themselves for the biggest share, and they made Imbry's stomach turn.

They were even worse than most of the TSN officers and men he'd known.

"Imbry."

He looked up. Lindenhoff was standing, arms akimbo, under the schematic at the head of the briefing room.

"Yes?" Imbry answered tightly.

"You take II. It's a rainforest world. Humanoid inhabited."

"I've studied the surveys."

Lindenhoff's heavy mouth twitched. "I hope so. You're going alone. There's nothing the natives can do to you that you won't be able to handle. Conversely, there's nothing much of any value on the planet. You'll contact the natives and try to get them started on some kind of civilization. You'll explain what the Terran Union is, and the advantages of trade. They ought to be able to grow some luxury agricultural products. See how they'd respond toward developing a technology. If Coogan turns up with some industrial ores on IV, they'd make a good market, in time. That's about the general idea. Nobody expects you to accomplish much—just push 'em in the right direction. Take two weeks. All straight?"

"Yes." Imbry felt his jaws tightening. Something for nothing again. First the Corporation developed a market, then it sold it the ores it found on a neighboring world.

No, he wasn't angry about having been given an assignment that couldn't go wrong and that wouldn't matter much if it did. He was quite happy about it, because he intended to do as little for the Corporation as he could.

"All right, that's about it, boys," Lindenhoff finished up. He stepped off the platform and the lights above the schematic went out. "You might as well draw your equipment and get started. The quicker it all gets done, the quicker we'll get paid."

Coogan slapped him on the back as they walked out on the flight deck. "Remember what I said," he chuckled. "If there's any ambition in the gooks at all, shove it hard. Me, I'm going to be looking mighty hard for something to sell 'em."

"Yeah, sure!" Imbry snapped.

Coogan looked at him wide-eyed. "What's eating you, boy?"

Imbry took a deep breath. "You're eating me, Coogan. You and the rest of the set-up." He stopped and glared tensely at Coogan. "I signed a contract. I'll do what I'm obligated to. But I'm getting off this ship when I come back, and if I ever hear about you birds again, I'll spit on the sidewalk when I do."

Coogan reddened. He took a step forward, then caught himself and dropped his hands. He shook his head. "Imbry, I've been watching you go sour for the last week. All right, that's the breaks. Old Smiley made a mistake. It's not the first time—and you could have fooled me, too, at first. What's your gripe?"

"What d'you think it is? How about Lindenhoff's giving you Petrick for a partner?"

Coogan shook his head again, perplexed. "I don't follow you. He's a geologist, isn't he?"

Imbry stared at him in astonishment. "You don't follow me?" Coogan was the one who'd told him about Petrick's drinking. He remembered the patronizing lift to Coogan's lips as he looked across the lounge at the white-faced, muddy-eyed man walking unsteadily through the room.

"Let's move along," Lindenhoff said from behind them.

Imbry half-turned. He looked down at the Assignment Officer in surprise. He hadn't heard the man coming. Neither had Coogan. Coogan nodded quickly.

"Just going, Lindy." Throwing another baffled glance at Imbry, he trotted across the deck toward his sub-ship, where Petrick was standing and waiting.

"Go on, son," Lindenhoff said. "You're holding up the show."

Imbry felt the knotted tension straining at his throat. He snatched up his pack.

"All right," he said harshly. He strode over to his ship, skirting out of the way of the little trucks that were humming back and forth around the ships, carrying supplies and maintenance crewmen. The flight deck echoed back to the clangs of slammed access hatches, the crash of a dropped wrench, and the soft whir of truck motors. Maintenance men were running back and forth, completing final checks, and armorers struggled with the heavy belts of ammunition being loaded into the guns on Jusek's ship. In the harsh glare of work lights, Imbry climbed up through his hatch, slammed it shut, and got up into his control compartment.

The ship was a slightly converted model of the standard TSN carrier scout.

He fingered the controls distastefully. Grimacing, he jacked in his communication leads and contacted the tower for a check. Then he set up his flight plan in the ballistic computer, interlocked his AutoNav, and sat back, waiting.

Lindenhoff and his fearsome scar. Souvenir of danger on a frontier world? Badge of courage? Symbol of intrepidness?

Actually, he'd gotten it when a piece of scaffolding fell on him during a production of *A Midsummer Night's Dream*, well before he ever came aboard the *Sainte Marie*.

The flight deck cleared. Imbry set his ship's circulators. The flight deck alarm blasted into life.

The deck canopy slid aside, and the flight deck's air billowed out into space. Imbry energized his main drive.

"Imbry clear for launch."

"Check, Imbry. Launch in ten."

He counted down, braced back against his couch. The catapult rammed him up off the deck, and he fired his engines. He rose high above the *Sainte Marie*, hovering, and then the ship nosed down and he trailed a wake of fire across the spangled night, in toward the foreign sun.

CHAPTER II

Almost from pole to pole, World II was the deep, lush color of rainforest vegetation. Only at the higher latitudes was it interspersed with the surging brown-green of prairie grass and bush country, tapering into something like a temperate ecology at the very "top" and "bottom" of the planet. Where there was no land, there was the deeper, bluer green of the sea. And on the sea, again, the green of islands.

Imbry balanced his ship on end, drifting slowly down. He wanted a good look and a long look.

His training in the TSN had fitted him admirably for this job. Admirably enough so that he depended more on his own observation than he did on the aerial survey results, which had been fed raw into a computer and emerged as a digested judgment on the planet's ecology and population, and the probable state and nature of its culture. The TSN applied this judgment from a military standpoint. The Corporation applied it to contact work. Imbry's experience had never known it to go far wrong. But he distrusted things mechanical, and so he hung in the sky for an hour or more, checking off promising-looking sites as they passed under him—and giving his bitterness and disillusion time to evaporate.

Down there was a race that had never heard of any people but itself; a race to which large portions of even its own planet must be unknown and enigmatic. A fairly happy race, probably. And if the Corporation found no significance in that, Imbry did. He was going to be their first touch with the incredible vastness in which they floated, and whatever he could do to smooth the shock and make their future easier, he meant to do, to the best of his ability. And if the Corporation had no feelings, he did. If there was no idealism aboard the *Sainte Marie*, there was some in him.

Finally, he picked an area on the eastern shore of the principal continent, and drifted down toward it, slipping in over the swelling expanse of an island-speckled ocean. Following the curve of a chain of atolls extending almost completely across the sea, he lost altitude steadily, finding it possible, now, with some of the tension draining out of him, to enjoy the almost effortless drift through the quiet sky, and the quick responsiveness of his ship. It wasn't quite as he'd dreamed it, but it was good. The mother ship was far away, and here on this world he was alone, coming down just above the tops of the breakers, now, settling gently on a broad and gleaming beach.

The anchoring field switched on, and bored down until it found bedrock. The sand around the ship pressed down in a shallow depression. Imbry turned away from the beach and began to walk into the jungle, his detectors and pressor fields tingling out to all sides of him. He walked slowly in the direction of a village, wearing his suit with its built-in equipment, with his helmet slung back between his shoulder blades.

The jungle was typical rainforest. There were trees which met the climatic conditions, and therefore much resembled ordinary palms. The same was true of the thick undergrowth, and, from the sound of them, of the avian fauna. The chatter in the trees was not quite as harsh as the Terrestrial version, nor as shrill. From the little he'd seen, that seemed typical—a slightly more leisurely, slightly gentler world than the Pacific belt of Earth. He walked slowly, as much from quiet enjoyment as from caution. Overhead, the sky was a warm blue, with soft clouds hanging over the atolls at the horizon. The jungle ran with bright color and deep, cool green. Imbry's face lost its drawn-up tension, and his walk became relaxed.

He found a trail in a very short time, and began following it, trusting to his detectors and not looking around except in simple curiosity. And quite soon after that, his detector field pinged, and the pressor pushed back against the right side of his chest. He turned it down, stopped, and looked in that direction. The field was set for sentient life only, and he knew he was about to meet his first native. He switched on his linguistic computer and waited.

The native, when he stepped out on the trail, was almost humanoid enough to pass for a Terrestrial. His ears were set a bit differently, and his musculature was not quite the same. It was also impossible to estimate his age, for none of the usual Terrestrial clues were applicable. But those were the only differences Imbry could see. His skin was dark enough so there was no mistaking him for a Caucasian—if you applied human standards—but a great deal of that might be simple suntan. His hair was light brown, grew out of his scalp in an ordinary fashion, and had been cut. He was wearing a short, skirt-like garment, with a perfectly ordinary navel showing above it in a flat stomach. The pattern of his wraparound was of the blocky type to which woven cloth is limited, and it was bright, in imitation of the forms and colors available in the jungle.

He looked at Imbry silently, out of intelligent black eyes, with a tentative smile on his mouth. He was carrying nothing in his open hands, and he seemed neither upset nor timid.

Imbry had to wait until he spoke first. The computer had to have something to work with. Meanwhile, he smiled back. His TSN training had prepared him for situations exactly like this. In exercises, he'd duplicated this situation a dozen times, usually with ET's much more fearsome and much less human. So he merely smiled back, and there was no tension or misgiving in the atmosphere at all. There was only an odd, childlike shyness, which, once broken, could only lead to an invitation to come over to the other fellow's house.

The native's smile broadened, and he raised one hand in greeting, breaking into soft, liquid speech that seemed to run on and on without stopping, for many syllables at a time.

The native finished, and Imbry had to wait for his translator to make up its mind. Finally, it whispered in his ear.

"This is necessarily a rough computation. The communication is probably: 'Hello. Are you a god?' (That's an approximation. He means something between 'ancestor' and 'deity'.) 'I'm very glad to meet you.'"

Imbry shook his head at the native, hoping this culture didn't take that to mean "yes". "No," he said to the computer, "I'm an explorer. And I'm glad to meet you." He continued to smile.

The computer hummed softly. "'Explorer' is inapplicable as yet," it told Imbry. It didn't have the vocabulary built up.

The native was looking curiously at the little box of the computer sitting on Imbry's shoulder. His jungle-trained ears were sharp, and he could obviously hear at least the sibilants as it whispered. His curiosity was friendly and intelligent; he seemed intrigued.

"All right, try: 'I'm like you. Hello,'" Imbry told the computer.

The translator spoke to the native. He looked at Imbry in gentle unbelief, and answered.

This time, it was easier. The translator sank its teeth into this new material, and after a much shorter lag, without qualification, gave Imbry the native's communication, in its usual colloquial English, somewhat flavored:

"Obviously, you're not like me very much. But, we'll straighten that out later. Will you stay in my village for a while?"

Imbry nodded, to register the significance of the gesture. "I'd be glad to. My name's Imbry. What's yours?"

"Good. I'm Tylus. Will you walk with me? And who's the little ancestor on your shoulder?"

Imbry walked forward, and the native waited until they were a few feet apart and then began leading the way down the trail.

"That's not an ancestor," Imbry tried to explain. "It's a machine that changes your speech into mine and mine into yours." But the translator broke down completely at that. The best it could offer to do was to tell Tylus that it was a lever that talked. And "your speech" and "my speech" were concepts Tylus simply did not have.

In all conscience, Imbry had to cancel that, so he contented himself with saying it was not an ancestor. Tylus immediately asked which of Imbry's respected ancestors it would be if it *were* an ancestor, and it was obvious that the native regarded Imbry as being, in many respects, a charming liar. But it was also plain that charming liars were accorded due respect in Tylus's culture, so the two were fairly well acquainted by the time they reached the outskirts of the village, and there was no longer any lag in translation at all.

The village was built to suit the environment. The roofs and walls of the light, one-room houses were made of woven frond mats tied down to a boxy frame. Every house had a porch for socializing with passersby, and a cookfire out front. Most of the houses faced in on a circular village square, with a big, communal cooking pit for special events, and the entire village was set in under the trees just a little away from the shoreline. There were several canoes on the sand above high water, and at some time this culture had developed the outrigger.

There was a large amount of shouting back and forth going on among the villagers, and a good-sized crowd had collected at the point where the trail opened out into the village clearing. But Tylus urged Imbry forward, passing proudly through the crowd, and Imbry went with him, feeling somewhat awkward about it, but not wanting to leave Tylus marching on alone. The villagers moved aside to let him through, smiling, some of them grinning at Tylus's straight back and proudly carried head, none of them, obviously, wanting to deprive their compatriot of his moment.

Tylus stopped when he and Imbry reached the big central cooking pit, turned around, and struck a pose with one arm around Imbry's shoulders.

"Hey! Look! I've brought a big visitor!" Tylus shouted, grinning with pleasure.

The villagers let out a whoop of feigned surprise, laughing and shouting congratulations to Tylus, and cordial welcomes to Imbry.

"He *says* he's not a god!" Tylus climaxed, giving Imbry a

broad, sidelong look of grinning appreciation for his ability to be ridiculous. " He came out of a big *lhoni* egg on the beach, and he's got a father-ghost who sits on his shoulder in a little black pot and gives him advice! "

" Oh, that's ingenious! " someone in the crowd commented in admiration.

" Look how fair he is! " one of the women exclaimed.

" Look how much handsomer than us he is! "

" Look how richly he's dressed! Look at the jewels shining in his silver belt! "

Imbry's translator raced to give him representative crowd comments, and he grinned back at the crowd. His rescue training had always presupposed grim, hostile or at best non-committal ET's that would have to be persuaded into helping him locate the crashed personnel of the stricken ship. Now, the first time he'd put it to actual use, he found reality giving theory a bland smile, and he sighed and relaxed completely. Once he'd disabused this village of its god-notions in connection with him, he'd be able to not only work but be friendly with these people. Not that they weren't already cordial.

He looked around at the crowd, both to observe it and to give everybody a look at his smile.

The crowd was composed, in nearly equal parts, of men and women very much like Tylus, with no significant variation except for age and sex characteristics that ranged from the appreciable to the only anthropologically interesting. In lesser part, there were children, most of them a little timid, some of them awestruck, all of them naked.

An older man, wearing a necklace of carved wood in addition to his wraparound, came forward through the crowd. Imbry had to guess at his age, but he thought he had it fairly accurately. The native had white hair, for one thing, and a slight thickness to his waist. For another, he was rather obviously the village head man, and that indicated age, and the experience it brought with it.

The head man raised his arm in greeting, and Imbry replied.

" I am Iano. Will you stay with us in our village? "

Imbry nodded. "My name's Imbry. I'd like to stay here for a while."

Iano broke into a smile. "Fine! We're all very glad to meet you. I hope your journey can be interrupted for a long time." He smiled. "Well, if you say you're not a god, who do you say you are?" There was a ripple of chuckling through the crowd.

"I'm a man," Imbry answered. The translator had meanwhile worked out the proper wording for what he wanted to say next. "I'm an explorer from another country." The local word, of course, was not quite "explorer"—it was "traveler-from - other - places - for - the - enjoyment - of - it - and - to - see - what - I - can - find."

Iano chuckled. Then gravely, he asked: "Do you always travel in an *lhoni* egg, Imbry-who-says-he-is-Imbry?"

Imbry chuckled back in appreciation of Iano's shrewdness. He was enjoying this, even if it was becoming more and more difficult to approach the truth.

"That's no *lhoni* egg," he deprecated with a broad gesture to match. "That's only my . . ." And here the translator had to give up and render the word as "canoe".

Iano nodded with a gravity so grave it was obviously no gravity at all. Tylus, standing to one side, gave Imbry a look of total admiration at this effort which overmatched all his others.

"Ah. Your canoe. And how does one balance a canoe shaped like an *lhoni* egg?"

Imbry realized what the translator had had to do. He'd been afraid of as much. He searched for the best answer, and the best answer seemed to be to tell the truth and stick to it. These people were intelligent. If he presented them with a consistent story, and backed it up with as much proof as he could muster, they'd eventually see that nothing so scrupulously self-consistent could possibly be anything but the truth.

"Well," he said slowly, wondering what the effect would be at first, "it's a canoe that doesn't sail on water. It sails in the sky."

There was a chorus of admiration through the crowd. As much of it seemed to be meant for Iano as for Imbry. They appeared to think Imbry had made a damaging admission in this contest.

Iano smiled. "Is your country in the sky?"

Imbry struggled for some way of making it understandable. "Yes and no," he said carefully. "It's necessary to travel through the sky to get to my country, but when you get there you're in a place that's very much like here, in some ways."

Iano smiled again. "Well, of course. How else would you be happy if there weren't places like this to live, in the sky?"

He turned toward the other villagers. "He *said* he wasn't a god," he declared quietly, his eyes twinkling.

There was a burst of chuckling, and now all the admiring glances were for Iano.

The head man turned back to Imbry. "Will you stay in my house for a while? We will produce a feast later in the day."

Imbry nodded gravely. "I'd be honored." The villagers were smiling at him gently as they drifted away, and Imbry got the feeling that they were being polite and telling him that his discomfiture didn't really matter.

"Don't be sad," Tylus whispered. "Iano's a remarkably shrewd man. He could make anybody admit the truth. I'm quite sure that when he dies, he'll be some kind of god himself."

Then he waved a hand in temporary farewell and moved away, leaving Imbry alone with the gravely smiling Iano.

CHAPTER III

Imbry sat on the porch with Iano. Both of them looked out over the village square, sitting side by side. It seemed to be the expected posture for conversation between a god and someone who was himself a likely candidate for a similar position, and it certainly made for ease of quiet contemplation before each new sentence was brought out into words.

Imbry was still wearing his suit. Iano had politely suggested that he might be warm in it, but Imbry had explained.

"It cools me. That's only one of the things it does. For one thing, if I took it off I wouldn't be able to talk to you. In my country we have different words."

Iano had thought about it for a moment. Then he said: "Your wraparound must have powerful ancestors living in it." He thought a moment more. "Am I right in supposing that this is a new attribute you're trying out, and it hasn't grown up enough to go about without advice?"

Imbry'd been glad of several minutes in which to think. Then he'd tried to explain.

"No," he said, "the suit (perforce, the word was 'wrap-around-for-the-whole-body') was made—was built—by other men in my country. It was built to protect me, and to make me able to travel anywhere without being in any danger." But that was only just as much as repeating Iano's theory back to him in different form, and he realized it after Iano's polite silence had extended too long to be anything but an answer in itself.

He tried to explain the concept "machine".

"I'll teach you a new word for a new thing," he said.

Iano nodded attentively.

Imbry switched off the translator, making sure Iano saw the motion and understood the result. Then he repeated "machine" several times, and, once Iano had accustomed himself to Imbry's new voice, which up to now he'd only heard as an indistinct background murmur to the translator's speaker, the head man picked it up quickly.

"Mahschin," he said at last, and Imbry switched his translator back on. "Go on, Imbry."

"A machine is a number of levers, working together. It is built by perfectly ordinary artisans—not gods, Iano, but men like yourself and myself—who have a good deal of knowledge and skill. With one lever, you can raise a tree trunk. With many levers, shaped into paddles, men can push the tree through the water, after they have shaped it into a canoe.

"So a machine is like the many levers that move the canoe. But usually it doesn't need men to push it. It goes on by itself, because it—"

Here he had to stop for a minute. These people had no concept of storing energy and then releasing it to provide motive power. Iano waited, patient and polite

"It has a little bit of fire in it," Imbry was forced to say lamely. "Fire can be put in a box—in something like two pots fastened tightly on top of each other—so that it can't get out. But it wants to get out—it pushes against the inside of the two pots—so if you make a hole in the pots and put a lever in the way, the fire rushing out pushes the lever."

He looked at Iano, but couldn't make out whether he was being believed or not. Half the time, he had no idea what kind of almost-but-sadly-not-quite concepts the translator might be substituting for the things he was saying.

"A machine can be built to do almost anything that would otherwise require a lot of men. For instance, I could have brought another man with me who was skilled at learning words that weren't his. Then I wouldn't need the little black pot, which is a machine that learns words that aren't the same as mine. But the machine does it faster, and in some ways, better."

He stopped, hoping Iano had understood at least part of it.

After a time, Iano nodded gravely. "That's very ingenious. It saves your ancestors the inconvenience of coming with you and fatiguing themselves. I had no idea such a thing could be done. But of course, in your country there are different kinds of fires than we have here."

Which was a perfectly sound description, Imbry had to admit, granting Iano's viewpoint.

So now they'd been sitting quietly for a number of minutes, and Imbry had begun to realize that he might have to work for a long time before he extricated himself from this embarrassment. Finally he said, "Well, if you think I'm a god, what kind of a god do you think I am?"

Iano answered slowly. "Well, to tell you the truth, I don't know. You might be an ancestor. Or you might be only a man who has made friends with a lot of his ancestors." Imbry felt a flash of hope, but Iano went on: "Which, of course, would make you a god. Or—" He paused, and Imbry, taking a sideward look, caught Iano looking at him cautiously. "Or you might be no ancestor and no man-god. You might be one of the very-real-gods. You might be the cloud god, or the jungle god, taking the attribute of a man. Or . . . you might be *the* god. You might be the-father-of-all-*lhoni*."

Imbry took a deep breath. "Would you describe the *lhoni* to me, please," he said.

"Certainly." Iano's voice and manner were still cautious. "The *lhoni* are animals which live in the sea or on the beaches, as they choose. They leave their eggs on the beaches, but they rear their young in the sea. They are fishers, and they are very wise. Many of them are ancestors." He said it with unusual respect and reverence.

Imbry sat quietly again. The god who was the-father-of-all-the-*lhoni* would not only be the father of many ancestors, who were themselves minor gods, he would also control the sea, everything pertaining to the sea, the beaches, probably all the islands, and the fates of those whose lives were tied to the sea, who were themselves fishers, like the villagers. Imbry wondered how much geography the villagers knew. They might consider that the land was always surrounded by ocean—that, as a matter of fact, the universe consisted of ocean encircling a relatively small bit of land.

If Iano thought that was who Imbry might be, then he might very well be thinking that he was in the presence of the greatest god there was. A typical god, of course—there wasn't a god in the world who didn't enjoy a joke, a feast, and a good untruth-for-the-fun-of-everybody at least as much as anybody else—but still, though you might not expect too much of the household lares and penates, when it came to Jupiter himself . . .

Imbry couldn't let that go on. Almost anything might happen. He might leave a religion behind him that, in a few generations of distortion, might twist itself—and the entire culture—into something monstrous. He might leave the way open for the next Corporation man to practice a brand of exploitation that would be near to unimaginable.

Imbry remembered what the *conquistadores* had done in Central and South America, and his hackles rose.

"No!" he exploded violently, and Iano recoiled a little, startled. "No, I'm not a god. Not any kind. I'm a man—a different kind of man, maybe, but just a man. The fact that I have a few machines doesn't prove anything. The fact that I know more about some things than you do doesn't prove anything. I come from a country where the people can keep records, so nothing's lost when a man who has some wisdom dies. I've been taught out of those records, and I'm helped by machines built by other men who study other records. But do you think my people are any better than yours? You think the men I have to work with are good, or brave, or kind? No more than you. Less. We kill each other, we take away from other people what isn't ours, we lie—we tell untruths-for-unfair-advantage—we leave bad where we found good—we're just men, we're not anything like gods, and we never will be!"

Iano had recovered his composure quickly. He nodded.

"No doubt," he said. "No doubt, to one god other gods are much like other men are to a man. Possibly even gods have gods. But that is not for us to say. We are men *here,* not in the country of the gods. There is the jungle, the sky, and the sea. And those who know more places than that must be our gods." He looked at Imbry with quick sympathy. "It's sad to know that even a god must be troubled."

CHAPTER IV

The odds were low that any of the food served at the feast could hurt him. Aside from the fact that the ecology was closely parallel to Earth's, Imbry's system was flooded with Antinfect from the precautionary shot he'd gotten aboard the mother ship. But he couldn't afford to take the chance of getting sick. It might help destroy the legend gathered around him, but it would also leave him helpless. He had too much to do in too short a time to risk that. So he politely faked touching his tongue to each of the dishes as it was passed to him, and settled for a supper of rations out of his suit, grimacing as he heard someone whisper behind him that the god had brought his own god-food with him because the food of men could not nourish him in this attribute.

No matter what he did, he couldn't shake the faith of the villagers. It was obvious at a glance that he was a god; therefore, *ipso facto*, everything he did was god-like.

He sat beside Iano and his wives, watching the fire roar in the communal pit and listening to the pounding beat of the musicians, but, even though the villagers were laughing happily and enjoying themselves immensely, he could not recapture the mood of easy relaxation he had borrowed from them and their world this afternoon. The *Sainte Marie* pressed too close to him. When he left here, he'd never be able to come back—and a ravaged world would haunt him for the rest of his life.

"Hey! Imbry! Look what I've got to show you!"

He looked up, and there was Tylus, coming toward him hand-in-hand with a quietly beautiful girl, and holding a baby just into the toddling stage. The child was being half-led, half-dragged, and seemed to be enjoying it.

Imbry smiled broadly. There was no getting away from it. Tylus enjoyed life so hugely that nobody near him could quite escape the infection.

"This is my woman, Pia," Tylus said with a proud grin, and the girl smiled shyly. "And this one hasn't got his name yet." He reached down and slapped the baby playfully, and the boy grinned from ear to ear.

Everyone around the fire chuckled. Imbry grinned despite himself, and nodded gravely to Tylus. "I'm glad to meet them." He smiled at Pia. "She must have been blind to pick you when she could have had so much better." The girl blushed, and everyone burst into laughter, while Tylus postured in proud glee. Imbry nodded toward the boy. "If he didn't look so much like his father, I'd say he was a fine one."

There was fresh laughter, and Imbry joined in it because he almost desperately needed to; but after it trailed away and Tylus and his family were gone back into their hut, after the fire died and the feast was over, when Imbry lay on the mat in Iano's house and the wind clashed the tree fronds while the surf washed against the beach—then Imbry lay tightly awake.

Given time—given a year or two—he might be able to break down the villagers' idea about him. But he doubted it. Iano was right. Even if he threw away his suit and left himself with no more equipment than any of the villagers possessed, he knew too much. Earth and the Terran Union were his heritage, and that was enough to make a god of any man among these people. If he so much as introduced the wheel into his culture, he was doing something none of these people had conceived of in all their history.

And he had nothing like a year. In two weeks' time, even using eidetic techniques, he could barely build up enough of a vocabulary in their language to do without his translator for simpler conversations. And, again, it wouldn't make a particle of difference whether he spoke their language or not. Words would never convince them.

But he had to get through to them somehow.

The cold fact was that during a half day's talk, he hadn't gotten anyone in the village to take literally even the slightest thing he said. He was a god. Gods speak in allegories, or gods proclaim laws. Gods do not speak man-to-man. And if they do, rest assured it is part of some divine plan, designed to meet inscrutable ends by subtle means.

What was it Lindenhoff had told him?

"You'll contact the natives and try to get them started on some kind of civilization. You'll explain what the Terran Union is, and the advantages of trade. See how they'd respond toward developing a technology."

It couldn't be done. Not by a god who might, at worst, be only a demi-god, who might at best even be *the* god, and who could not, under any circumstances, possibly be considered on a par with the other travelers-for-pleasure who occasionally turned up from over the sea but who were manifestly only other men.

He wasn't supposed to be a stern god, or an omnipotent god, or a being above the flesh. That kind of deity took a monotheist to appreciate him. He was simply supposed to be a god of these people—vain and happily boastful at times, a liar at times, a glutton at times, a drunkard at times, timid at times, adventurous at times, a hero at times, and heir to other sins of the flesh at other times, but always powerful, always above the people in wisdom of his own kind, always a god: always a mute with a whispering ancestor on his shoulder.

But if he felt them now, they'd be lost. Someone else would come down, and be a god. Kenton, or Ogin, or Maguire the killer. And when the new god realized the situation, he'd stop trying to make these people into at least some kind of rudimentary market. They wouldn't even have that value to turn them into an interest to be protected. Lindenhoff would think of something else to do with them, for the Corporation's good. Turn them into a labor force for the mines Coogan would be opening up on IV, perhaps. Or else enslave them here. Have the god nudge them into becoming farmers for the luxury market, or introduce a technology whether they understood it or not.

That might work. If the god and his fellow gods found stones for them to dig and smelt into metal, and showed them how to make machines, they might do it.

To please the god by following his advice. Not because they understood or wanted machines—or needed them—but to fulfill the god's inscrutable plan. They'd sicken with the bewilderment in their hearts, and lose their smiles in the smelter's heat. The canoes would rot on the beaches, and the fishing spears would break. The houses would crumble on the ocean's edge until the sea reached up and swept the village clean, and the *lhoni* eggs would hatch out in the warming sun. The village would be gone, and its people slaving far away, lonesome for their ancestors.

He had to do it. Somehow, within these two weeks, he had to give them a chance of some kind.

It would be his last chance, too. Twenty-six years of life, and all of it blunted. He was failing here, with the taste of the Corporation bitter in his mouth. He'd found nothing in the TSN but brutal officers and cynical men waiting for a war to start somewhere, so the promotions and bonuses would come, and meanwhile making the best they could out of what police actions and minor skirmishes there were with weak alien races. Before that, school, and a thousand timemarkers and campus wheels for everyone who thought that some day, if he was good enough, he'd have something to contribute to Mankind.

The god had to prove to be human after all. And the human could talk to these other men, as just another man, and then perhaps they might advance of themselves to the point where they could begin a civilization that was part of them, and part of some plan of theirs, instead of some god's. And someday these people, too, would land their metal canoes on some foreign beach under a foreign sun.

He had to destroy himself. He had to tear down his own façade.

Just before he fell into his fitful sleep, he made his decision. At the first opportunity to be of help in some way they would consider more than manlike, he'd fail. The legend would crumble, and he could be a man.

He fell asleep, tense and perspiring, and the stars hung over the world, with the mother ship among them.

CHAPTER V

The chance came. He couldn't take it.

Two days had gone by, and nothing had happened to change the situation. He spent two empty days talking to Iano and as many other villagers as he could, and the only knowledge they gained was an insight into the ways of gods, who proved, after all, to be very much like men, on their own grander scale. One or two were plainly saddened by his obvious concern over something they, being unfortunately only men, could not quite grasp. Iano caught something of his mood, and was upset by it until his face fell into a puzzled, concerned look that was strange to it. But it only left him and Imbry further apart. There was no bridge between them.

On the third day, the sea was flat and oily, and the air lay dankly still across the village. The tree fronds hung down limply, and the clouds thickened gradually during the night, so that Imbry woke up to the first sunless day he'd seen. He got up as quietly as he could, and left Iano's house, walking slowly across the compound toward the sea. He stood on the beach, looking out across the glassy swells, thinking back to the first hour in which he'd hung above that ocean and slowly come down with the anticipation burning out the disgust in him.

He threw a shell as far out into the water as he could, and watched it skip once, skip twice, teeter in the air, and knife into the water without a splash. Then he turned around and walked slowly back into the village, where one or two women were beginning to light their cookfires.

He greeted them listlessly, and they answered gravely, their easy smiles dying. He wandered over toward Tylus's house. And heard Pia crying.

"Hello!"

Tylus came out of the house, and for the first time Imbry saw him looking strained, his lips white at the corners. "Hello, Imbry," he said in a tired voice.

"What's wrong, Tylus?"

Tylus shrugged. "The baby's going to die."

Imbry stared up at him. "Why?"

"He cut his foot yesterday morning. I put a poultice on it. It didn't help. His foot's red today, and it hurts him to touch it. It happens."

"Oh, no, it doesn't. Not any more. Let me look at him." Imbry came up the short ladder to Tylus's porch. "It can't be anything I can't handle."

He knew the villagers' attitude toward death. Culturally, death was the natural result of growing old, of being born weak, and, sometimes, of having a child. Sometimes, too, a healthy person could suddenly get a pain in the belly, lie in agony for a day, and then die. Culturally, it usually made the victim an ancestor, and grief for more than a short time was something the villagers were too full of living to indulge in.

But sometimes it was harder to take; in this tropical climate, a moderately bad cut could infect like wildfire, and then someone died who didn't seem to have been ready for it.

Tylus's eyes lit up for a moment. Then they became gravely steady.

"You don't have to, if you don't want to, Imbry. Suppose some other god wants him? Suppose his ancestors object to your stepping in? And—and besides—" Tylus dropped his eyes. "I don't know. Maybe you're not a god."

Imbry couldn't stop to argue. "I'd like to look at him anyway. No matter what might happen."

The hopelessness drained out of Tylus's face. He touched Imbry's arm. "Come into my house," he said, repeating the social formula gratefully. "Pia! Imbry's here to make the baby well!"

Imbry strode into the house, pulling his medkit out of his suit. Pia turned away from the baby's mat, raising her drawn face. Then she jumped up and went to stand next to Tylus, clenching his hand.

The baby was moving his arms feverishly, and his cheeks were flushed. But he'd learned, through the night, not to move the bandaged foot.

Imbry cut the scrap of cloth away with his bandage shears, wincing at the puffy, white-lipped gash. He snapped the pencil light out of its clip and took a good look into the wound.

It was dirty as sin, packed with some kind of herb mixture that was hopelesly embedded in the tissues. Cleaning it thoroughly was out of the question. Cursing softly, he did the best he could, not daring to try the anesthetic syrette in the kit. He had no idea of what even a human child's dosage might be.

He had to leave a lot of the poultice in the wound. Working as fast as he could, he spilled an envelope of antibiotics over the gash, slapped on a fresh bandage, and then stood up. Antipyretics were out. The boy'd have to have his fever. There was one gamble he had to take, but he was damned if he'd take any more. He held up the ampule of Antinfect.

"Universal Antitoxin" was etched into the glass. Well, it had better be.

He broke the seal and stabbed the tip of his hyposprayer through the diaphragm. He retracted carefully. It was a three cc ampule. About half of it ought to do. He watched the dial on the sprayer with fierce concentration, inching the knob around until it read "1.5", and yanking the tip out.

Muttering a prayer, he fired the Antinfect into the boy's leg. Then he sighed, re-packed his kit, and turned around.

"If I haven't killed him, he'll be all right." He gestured down at the bandage. "There's going to be a lot of stuff coming out of that wound. Let it come. Don't touch the bandage. I'll take another look at it in a few hours. Meanwhile, let me know if he looks like he's getting worse." He smiled harshly. "And let me know if he's getting better, too."

Pia was looking at him with an awestruck expression on her face. Tylus's glance clung to the medkit and then traveled up to Imbry's eyes.

"You are a god," he said in a whisper. "You are more than a god. You are the god of all other gods."

"I know," Imbry growled. "For good and all now, even if the boy dies. I'm a god now no matter what I do." He strode out of the house and out across the village square, walking in short, vicious strides along the beach until he was out of sight of the village. He stood for a long time, looking out across the gray sea. And then, with a crooked twist to his lips and a beaten hopelessness in his eyes, he walked back into the village because there was nothing else he could do.

Lord knew where the hurricane had been born. Somewhere down the chain of islands—or past them—the mass of air had begun to whirl. Born out of the ocean, it spun over the water for hundreds of miles, marching toward the coast.

The surf below the village sprang into life. It lashed along the strand in frothing, growling columns, and the *lhoni* eggs washed out of their nests and rolled far down the slope of the beach before the waves picked them up again and crushed them against the stones and shells.

The trees tore the edges of their fronds against each other, and the broken ends flew away on the wind. The birds in the jungle began to huddle tightly into themsclves.

"Your canoe," Iano said to Imbry as they stood in front of the head man's house.

Imbry shook his head. "It'll stand."

He watched the families taking their few essential belongings out of their houses and storing them inside the overturned canoes that had been brought high inland early in the afternoon.

"What about this storm? Is it liable to be bad?"

Iano shook his head noncommitally. "There're two or three bad ones every season."

Imbry grunted and looked out over the village square. Even if the storm smashed the houses flat, they'd be up again two days afterward. The sea and the jungle gave food, and the fronded trees gave shelter. He saw no reason why these people wanted gods in the first place.

He saw a commotion at the door of Tylus's house. Tylus and Pia stood in the doorway. Pia was holding the baby.

"Look! Hey! Look!" Tylus shouted. The other villagers turned, surprised.

"Hey! Come look at my baby! Come look at the boy Imbry made well!" But Tylus himself didn't follow his own advice. As the other villagers came running, forgetting the possessions piled beside the canoes, he broke through them and ran across the square to Imbry and Iano.

"He's fine! He stopped crying! His leg isn't hot any more, and we can touch it without hurting him!" Tylus shouted, looking up at Imbry.

Imbry didn't know whether to laugh or cry. He smiled with an agonized twist of his mouth. "I thought I told you not to touch that foot."

"But he's *fine*, Imbry! He's even laughing!" Tylus was gesturing joyfully. "Imbry—"

"Yes?"

"Imbry, I want a gift."

"A gift?"

"Yes. I want you to give him your name. When his naming day comes, I want him to call himself The Beloved of Imbry."

My God, Imbry thought, I've done it! I've saddled them with the legend of myself. He looked down at Tylus. "Are you sure?" he asked, feeling the words come out of his tight throat.

"I would like it very much," Tylus answered with sudden quietness.

And there was nothing Imbry could say but, "All right. When his naming day comes, if you still want to."

Tylus nodded. Then, obviously, he realized he'd run out of things to say and do. With Imbry the ancestor, or Imbry the man-with-many-powerful-ancestors; with Imbry the demi-god, he could have found something else to talk about. But this was Imbry, the god of all gods, and that was different.

"Well . . . I have to be with Pia. Thank you." He threw Imbry one more grateful smile, and trotted back across the square, to where the other villagers were clustered around Pia, talking excitedly and often looking with shy smiles in Imbry's direction.

It was growing rapidly darker. Night was coming, and the hurricane was trudging westward with it. Imbry looked at Iano, with his wraparound plastered against his body by the force of the wind and his face in the darkness under the overhanging porch roof.

"What'll you do when the storm comes?" Imbry asked.

Iano gestured indefinitely. "Nothing, if it's a little one. If it's bad, we'll get close to the trees, on the side away from the wind."

"Do you think it looks like it'll get bad?"

Iano gestured in the same way. "Who knows?" he said, looking at Imbry.

Imbry looked at him steadily. "I'm only a man. I can't make it better or worse. I can't tell you what it's going to be. I'm only a man, no matter what Tylus and Pia think."

Iano gestured again. "There are men. I know that much because I am a man. There may be other men, who are our ancestors and our gods, who in their turn have gods. And those gods may have greater gods. But I am a man, and I know what I see and what I am. Later, after I die and am an ancestor, I may know other men like myself, and call them men. But these people who are not yet ancestors"—he swept his arm in a gesture that encircled the village—"these people will call me a god, if I choose to visit them.

"To Tylus and Pia—and to many others—you are the god of all gods. To myself . . . I don't know. Perhaps I am too near to being an ancestor not to think there may be other gods above you. But," he finished, "they are not my gods. They are yours. And to me you are more than a man."

The hurricane came with the night, and the sea was coldly phosphorescent as it battered at the shore. The wind screamed invisibly at the trees. The village square was scoured clean of sand and stones, and the houses were groaning.

The villagers sat on the ground, resting their backs against the thrashing trees.

Imbry couldn't accustom himself to the constant sway. He stood motionless beside the tree that sheltered Iano, using his pressors to brace himself. He knew the villagers were looking at him through the darkness, taking it as one more proof of what he was, but that made no difference any longer. He faced into the storm, feeling the cold sting of the wind.

Lindenhoff would be overjoyed. And Maguire would grin coldly. Coogan would count his money, and Petrick would drink a solitary toast to the helpless suckers he could make do anything he wanted.

And Imbry? He let the cold spray dash against his face and didn't bother to wipe it off. Imbry was ready to quit.

The universe was made the way it was, and there was no changing it, whether to suit his ideas of what men should be or not. The legendary heroes of the human race—the brave, the brilliant, selfless men who broke the constant trail for the rest of Mankind to follow—must have been a very different breed from what the stories said they were.

A house crashed over on the far side of the village, and crunched apart. He heard a woman moan in brief fear, but then her man must have quieted her, for there was no further sound from any of the dim figures huddled against the trees around him.

The storm rose higher. For a half hour, Imbry listened to the houses tearing down, and felt the spray in his face thicken until it was like rain. The phosphorescent wall of surf crept higher on the beach, until he could see it plainly; a tumbling, ghostly mass in among the trees nearest the beach. The wind became a solid wall, and he turned up the intensity on his pressors. He had no way of knowing whether the villagers were making any sound or not.

He felt a tug at his leg, and bent down, turning off his pressors. Iano was looking up at him, his face distorted by the wind, his hair standing away from one side of his head. Imbry closed one arm around the tree.

"What?" Imbry bellowed into the translator, and the translator tried to bellow into Iano's ear.

"It . . . very . . . very bad . . . very . . . rain . . . no rain . . ."

The translator struggled to get the message through to Imbry, but the wind tore it to tatters.

"Yes, it's bad," Imbry shouted. "What was that about rain?"

"Imbry . . . when . . . rain . . ."

Clearly and distinctly, he heard a woman scream. There was a second's death for the wind. And then the rain and the sea came in among the trees together.

White, furious water tore at his legs and pushed around his waist. He gagged on salt. Coughing and choking, he tried to see what was happening to the villagers.

But he was cut off in a furious, pounding, sluicing mass of water pouring out of the sky at last, blind and isolated as he tried to find air to breathe. He felt it washing into his suit, filling its legs, weighing his feet down. He closed his helmet in a panic, spilling its water down over his head, and as he snapped it tight another wave raced through the trees to break far inland, and he lost his footing.

He tumbled over and over in the churning water, fumbling for his pressor controls. Finally he got to them, and snapped erect, with the field on full. The water broke against his faceplate, flew away, and he was left standing in a bubble of emptiness that exactly outlined the field. Sea water walled in from the ground to the height of his face, and the rain flooded it from above.

Blind inside his bubble, he waited for the morning.

He awoke to a dim light filtering through to him, and he looked up to see layer after layer of debris piled atop his bubble. It was still raining, but the solid cloudburst was over. There was still water on the ground, but it was only a few inches deep. He collapsed his field, and the pulped sticks and chips of wood fell in a shower on him. He threw back his helmet and looked around.

The water had carried him into the jungle at the extreme edge of the clearing where the village had stood and from where he was he could see out to the heaving ocean.

The trees were splintered and bent. They lay across the clearing, pinning down a few slight bits of wreckage. But almost all traces of the village were gone. Where the canoes with their household possessions had lain in an anchored row, there was nothing left.

Only a small knot of villagers stood in the clearing. Imbry tried to count them; tried to compare them to the size of the crowd that had welcomed him into the village, and stopped. He came slowly forward, and the villagers shrank back. Iano stepped out to meet him, and, slowly, Tylus.

"Iano, I'm sorry," Imbry said in a dull voice, looking around the ravaged clearing again. If he'd had any idea the hurricane could possibly be that bad, he would have called the mother ship for help. Lindenhoff would have fired into the storm and disrupted it, to save his potential slaves.

"Why did this happen, Imbry?" Iano demanded. "Why was this done to us?"

Imbry shook his head. "I don't know. A storm— Nobody can blame anything."

Iano clenched his fists.

"I did not ask during the whole day beforehand, though I knew what would happen. I did not even ask in the beginning of the storm. But when I knew the rain must come;

when the sea growled and the wind stopped, *then*, at last, I asked you to make the storm die. Imbry, you did nothing. You made yourself safe, and you did nothing. *Why was this done?*"

Iano's torso quivered with bunched muscles. His eyes blazed. "If you were who we believed you to be, if you made Tylus's boy well, why did you do this? *Why did you send the storm?*"

It was the final irony: apparently, if Iano had accepted Imbry as a man, he would have told him in advance how bad the storm was likely to be. . . .

Imbry shook his head. "I'm not a god, Iano," he repeated dully. He looked at Tylus, who was standing pale and bitter-eyed behind Iano.

"Are they safe, Tylus?"

Tylus looked silently over Imbry's shoulder, and Imbry turned his head to follow his glance. He saw the paler shape crushed around the trunks of a tree, one arm still gripping the boy.

"I must make a canoe," Tylus said in a dead voice. "I'll go on a long journey-to-leave-the-sadness-behind. I'll go where there aren't any gods like you."

"Tylus!"

But Iano clutched Imbry's arm, and he had to turn back toward the head mean.

"We'll all have to go. We can't ever stay here again." The grip tightened on Imbry's arm, and the suit automatically pressed it off. Iano jerked his arm away.

"The storm came because of you. It came to teach us something. We have learned it." Iano stepped back. "You're not a great god. You tricked us. You're a bad ancestor—you're sick—you have the touch of death in your hand."

"I never said I was a god." Imbry's voice was unsteady. "I told you I was only a man."

Tylus looked at him out of his dead eyes. "How can you possibly be a man like us? If you're not a god, then you're a demon."

Imbry's face twisted. "You wouldn't listen to me. It's not my fault you expected something I couldn't deliver. Is it my fault you couldn't let me be what I am?"

"We know what you are," Tylus said.

There wasn't anything Imbry could tell him. He slowly turned away from the two natives and began the long walk back to the sub-ship.

He finished checking the board and energizing his starting motors. He waited for a minute, and threw in his atmospheric drive.

The rumble of jet throats shook through the hull, and throbbed in the control compartment. The ship broke free, and he retracted the landing jacks.

The throttles advanced, and Imbry fled into the stars.

He sat motionless for several minutes. The memory of Tylus's lifeless voice etched itself into the set of his jaw and the backs of his eyes. It seemed impossible that it wouldn't be there forever.

There was another thing to do. He clicked on his communicator.

"This is Imbry. Get me Lindenhoff."

"Check, Imbry. Stand by."

He lay in the piloting couch, waiting, and when the image of Lindenhoff's face built up on the screen, he couldn't quite meet its eyes.

"Yeah, Imbry?"

He forced himself to look directly into the screen. "I'm on my way in, Lindenhoff. I ran into a problem. I'm dictating a full report for the files, but I wanted to tell you first—and I think I've got the answer."

Lindenhoff grinned slowly. "Okay, Fred."

Lindenhoff was waiting for him as he berthed the sub-ship aboard the *Sainte Marie*. Imbry climbed out and looked quietly at the man.

Lindenhoff chuckled. "You look exactly like one of our real veterans," he said. "A hot bath and a good meal'll take care of that." He chuckled again. "It will, too—it takes more than once around the track before this business starts getting you."

"So you figure I'll be staying on," Imbry said, feeling tireder and older than he ever had in his life. "How do you know I didn't make a real mess of it, down there?"

Lindenhoff chuckled. "You made it back in one piece, didn't you? That's the criterion, Fred. I hate to say so, but it is. No mess can possibly be irretrievable if it doesn't kill the man who made it. Besides—you don't know enough to tell whether you made any mistakes or not."

Imbry grunted, thinking Lindenhoff couldn't possibly know how much of an idiot he felt like, and how much he had on his conscience.

"Well, let's get to this report of yours," Lindenhoff said.

Imbry nodded slowly. They walked off the *Sainte Marie's* flight decks into the labyrinth of steel decks below.

CHAPTER VI

It was three seasons after the storm, and Tylus was still on his journey. One day he came to a new island and ran his canoe up on the beach. Perhaps here he wouldn't find Pia and the nameless boy waiting for him in the palm groves.

He walked up the sand, and triggered the alarm without knowing it.

Aboard the mother ship, Imbry heard it go off and switched the tight-beam scanner on. The intercom speaker over his head broke into a crackle.

"Fred? You got that one?"

"Uh-huh, Lindy. Right here."

"Which set-up is it?"

"88 on the B grid. It's that atoll right in the middle of the prevailing wind belt."

"I've got to hand it to you, Fred. Those little traps of yours are working like a charm."

Imbry ran his hand over his face. He knew what was going to happen to that innocent native, whoever he was. He'd come out of it a man, ready to take on the job of helping his people climb upward, with a lot of his old ideas stripped away.

Imbry's mouth jerked sideways, in the habitual gesture that was etching a deep groove in the skin of his face.

But he wouldn't be happy while he was learning. It was good for him—but there was no way for him to know that until he'd learned.

"How many this time?" Lindenhoff asked. "Coogan tells me they could use a lot of new recruits in a hurry, in that city they're building up north."

"Just one canoe," Imbry said, looking at the image on the scanner. "Small one, at that. Afraid it's only one man, Lindy." He moved the picture a little. "Yeah. Just one," He focussed the controls.

"It's him! Tylus! We've got Tylus!"

There was a short pause on the other end of the intercom circuit. Then Lindenhoff said: "Okay, okay. You've finally got your pet one. Now, don't muff things in the rush." He chuckled softly and switched off.

Imbry bent closer to the scanner, though there was no real necessity for it. From here on, the process was automatic, and as inevitable as an avalanche.

Imbry watched the protoplasmic robots on the island come hesitantly through the underbrush toward the beach.

On the island, Tylus stopped. There was a crackle in the shrubbery, and a small, diffident figure stepped out. Its expression was watchful, but friendly. It looked rather much like a man, except for its small size and the shade of its skin. Its eyes were intelligent. It looked trustful.

"Hello," Tylus said. "I'm Tylus."

The little native came forward. Others followed it, some more timid than the first, some smiling cordially. They kept casting glances at the magic tree-pod which could carry a man over the sea.

"Hello," the little native answered in a soft, liquid voice. "Are you an ancestor ghost or a god ghost?"

And Tylus began learning about Imbry.

CONTACT BETWEEN EQUALS

ALICIA CAME OVER to my daybed with a rustle of cotton and a whisper of silk, and bent over me with a breath of perfume. "Will? It's time. Are you awake, Will?"

Awake? Because I'd been lying there motionless, it hadn't occurred to her that I might be counting the chimes from the clock in its hand-rubbed wooden case on the mantel.

"Dr. Champley's here, Will."

"I know. I heard him drive up." I opened my eyes with a brush of lashes against the loosely-wound gauze that swathed my head, and let in the light.

The light was white. Alicia'd taught me during the past week—she'd played colored lights on the gauze, and taught me the names of the colors. We had also talked about perceptive, and about the perception of shape and texture from a distance; I'm sure Dr. Champley had outlined a program of education, to get me a little reoriented ahead of time.

Alicia had been surprised how easily it had gone. She ought not to have been. I'd listened to talking books all my life, and there was radio, of course. And forty years of hearing people in conversation around me. I was a graduate of Harvard Business School. I was a millionaire—five and six times the millionaire my father had been. That did not happen by accident. It could not have happened to a man who did not think intelligently, analytically, and systematically. I had an exact picture of the world, in one-to-one correspondence with the world perceived by the sighted. My reorientation would consist of no more than simple transposition from one system to the other.

Champley had gotten out of his car, parked on the gravel road fronting the cottage. He came up the flagstone steps to the porch, opened the screen door, crossed the porch, knocked briefly, opened the front door, and stepped briskly into the room. The screen door of the porch sighed shut on its air spring, and latched.

"Hello, Doctor," Alicia said.

"Good afternoon, Mrs. Schaeffer. Is Mr. Schaeffer awake?"

It was a long speech for him. I put it away in my mind, to flesh out what little I knew about him.

Up to now, he'd been little more than someone Alicia'd talked about a great deal; the famous, brilliant young surgeon who'd become interested in William Schaeffer's case, and who thought he could do something about it. I'd taken considerable thought on all the factors involved. But Champley had been all business during the brief examination in his office—a few gentle touches around the face, a lifting of my lids, a click of the unseen flashlight, a thoughtful grunt or two, and one muttered word: "Maybe."

No buttering up, no bedside manner. I'd liked that. All the other verdicts had come from men who went through elaborate lectures to hide their inability. And it was always definite: "Yes", or "No". The second had at least been right. The first had been humbug.

Well, Champley'd brought it off, as far as we could tell at the moment. Alicia said it had only taken an hour's operating time. I'd come out of anesthesia in the ambulance, leaving Champley's clinic, and the most difficult part of the whole business had been remembering not to move my eyes at all for thirty-six hours. The ambulance had brought Alicia and me to this lake cottage of Champley's, because it was nearer his clinic than any of my lodges. Alicia and I had spent the week here alone, without distractions, working toward this time.

Well, I thought, I'm here, and he's here, and I'm getting impatient. "Doctor?"

"Yes, Mr. Schaeffer. Right here." He came across the raffia rug in crêpe-soled shoes. He was wearing a tweed suit—a nubby tweed, that rubbed as he moved his arms and legs—and he smelled of aftershave lotion.

"You smelled like iodoform in your office." And he had not met me at his clinic. An anesthetist had put me under. I knew damnably little about him. Except, of course, for what Alicia had told me.

"Yes," he said. "Well, now, let's see what I look like." Bandage shears clicked in his hand. Alicia put her cool fingers on my shoulder.

There was a cold, greasy feeling of metal sliding along my cheek. The gauze pulled slightly. Then it lay limp across the bridge of my nose.

"Try to keep your eyes closed, Mr. Schaeffer. Just for the moment. Let the light come through the lids before you open them."

"All right." He lifted the gauze, and the light was pink. I lay quietly, gathering myself. I did not feel grossly excited. But all week I had been extremely restless and ill-at-ease. Perhaps I would not let myself feel excitement. Perhaps *this* was excitement. Now, of course, the feeling was strongest of all, with things approaching their climaxes.

I did not open my eyes until Champley asked me to. I opened them slowly, and all I saw at first were blurred colors. That was all rignt. All that was familiar. But there was the new business of focussing to be done, and that took some time. Binocular vision was something I understood in theory—though I had some rather distorted images of what a lens might be—but I had to teach myself control of the necessary muscles.

After that, I had to make for myself all the discoveries a baby makes—what human beings looked like, where my hands and feet were; all the momentous things. I made them. I made them slowly and carefully. Alicia and Champley were patient. Finally I felt sure of myself.

Alicia, it seemed, had yellow hair, and was wearing a green dress. Champley was rather taller than she. He had black hair, and his suit was brown. It was all rather strange, seeing things which had previously only occupied relative positions. But we got through it all, and easily enough.

I went outside with them, finally, wearing smoked glasses. I stood like a child with an open primer. "Mountains. Forest. Sky. Clouds. Lake. Cottage. Cliff."

The cottage was built out from the side of the steep slope, with only the front porch touching earth at the edge of the narrow road that led down to the lake. The remainder was supported on pilings. I was made uneasy by all these things, but I shuffled my feet on the gravel of the road and turned my head so the breeze crossed my cheek, and then I was comfortable.

We went back into the cottage, and I sat down on the edge of the daybed. I suppose I was feeling a certain bravado at my new skill. I searched over the room. Daybed here. Fireplace there, with clock. Chairs, table, another small table with a slick-faced box on it. "That would be a television set, wouldn't it?"

"Yes, but that's for another day," Champley said quickly. "We don't want too much strain." He opened a fresh package of gauze and brought out two eyepads. Aicia stood in the center of the room, her legs bathed by a bar of sunlight exactly as I had heard a similar scene described in a book. The impression generated by the author had been one of youth and warmth. Alicia . . . Well, Alicia.

"Wait," I said. "I want to talk to you both."

"Of course," Champley said. "But you can do that just as well with your eyes bandaged."

"No. I want to watch your faces move. Sit down together in front of me."

Alicia raised her eyebrows toward Champley. Champley did not change expression in response. He made a faint wet sound when he moved his tongue away from the roof of his mouth. He moved to one of the two chairs in front of the fireplace and swung it around. He moved the other for Alicia, and both of them sat down.

I looked from one to the other, and fastened my glance on Champley.

"Well, you delivered," I said. "That excuses a great deal. But I won't give you Alicia and a fee in addition. You'll have to be satisfied with just her."

I had, for the first time, the opportunity to see that situation in which a writer inevitably says: "A look of consternation passed between them, and they burst into furious bickering. They began denying their guilt vehemently, and, in the end, fell to blaming each other for having been careless."

Alicia disappointed me. She merely turned to Champley and said: "I told you he was smarter than either one of us." Champley shrugged as though it hardly mattered, though it took me a moment's thought to understand what it was he had done with his shoulders. He said nothing, and continued to watch me with his face in repose. I took that for a sign of confidence, and did not like it.

"Very well," I said, "we understand each other. I'm grateful for your skill, Champley. I trust your other patients will enable you to support Alicia. But I can't understand why you and she went to all this trouble. Or where it all profits her. Does she think a sighted man will live to a riper old age than a blind one? And if so—I repeat—where has all this profited her?"

I did not like their reaction pattern. Not at all. I stood up and began prowling about the room.

"Sit down, Will!" Alicia said nervously.

That was more like it. But, why now? "Why?"

"You're making me nervous."

"Why now? Why must I sit still? Why must my eyes be bandaged immediately? What will I see? Why does this cottage seem a great deal bigger from the outside than the living room, bedroom, bath and kitchen I know?"

A look passed between them. It might have been consternation. Apparently, it had paid me to watch my feet as I walked and so learn the visual length of my average stride. "What's behind the kitchen?" I walked toward it, and Champley was up facing me, his schooled control deteriorating far enough to let me see it was a panic move.

"There's nothing back there," he said.

And that, of course, was patently ridiculous. I pushed by him and strode into the kitchen. There was a clear space along the wall, between a white box that was the refrigerator and the sink with its dripping faucet. There were arcing scuff marks on the floor. There was a door there, without a handle, hidden in the butted planks of the paneling. I ran my hands over it. I found no way of opening it. Something on the other side, quite large, and breathing, rolled up and nudged against it. The planking creaked.

I turned quickly and went back into the living room. Alicia was tugging at the baseboard plug of the television set.

"Now, why," I said, "would that be the most important action you could take to keep me in ignorance?"

"It was *loose*, Will! I was pushing it back *in*!" she cried. She was practically out of control.

I shook my head. Alicia."

Champley tried to stop me from going to the television set. He was impelled to urgency, but I was William Schaeffer. I brushed him aside and clicked the left-hand switch. Alicia stepped back.

The screen blazed up. It was flat, uncolored, and I could not adjust to that immediately. I scarcely heard what noise the set might be making. There was something pictured on it that I had never seen before, naturally enough, moving something like a mouth. Once I had absorbed that, I could listen. ". . . going to get you," it—or, rather, another component of the set said. The delivery was calm, without much intonation.

Alicia turned the set off sharply. "That's enough, Will. You'll—you'll hurt your eyes."

I almost laughed. But I was also curious. "What was that thing, anyway?"

"A children's program," Champley said.

"Well, all right, but what, specifically, was that thing?"

"A monster," Alicia said irritably. "Please let Dr. Champley bandage your eyes now."

"A monster, eh?" An entire body of literature had suddenly come clear to me. "Fascinating." I turned the set on again.

"Champley," the monster promised in its unhurried tone, "I'm going to get you soon." Then the screen went blank.

I turned the set off and turned around.

"What a fantastic coincidence!" Champley said.

"Oh, it *couldn't* have said 'Champley'," Alicia exclaimed. "It must have been another name like it."

"It said 'Champley'," I told her. I went back to the daybed and sat down. "All this is very interesting."

"Oh, Will!" Alicia snapped. "Don't be ridiculous! It was some kind of a coincidence. You happened to tune in some children's program at just the right instant."

"And the monster was pronouncing just the right name? Odd. How many Champleys do you suppose there are?" I was not feeling much elation. Cats may enjoy cat-and-mouse. I am not a cat. What I wanted was information.

Champley said nothing. Alicia continued to pay out her pathetic rope:

"This whole thing is . . . insane! You know very well there aren't any real monsters, and, if there were, what would they be doing on television?"

"Communicating," I said. "Now. Doctor Champley. Why would a monster want to get you?"

"Nothing's going to get me," Champley said.

"No doubt you think so," I said. "But you have already been proven a less effective human being than myself. I have no doubt there are other things in the Universe, as well, that could best you. The question is, where do I fit into your escape plan?"

And where did he meet his monster, and what had he done to incur its enmity? And so forth. But, first of all, why did he need me, why did he need me completely functional, and what did it profit Alicia?

I went quickly into the bedroom, and located the bureau by touch, with my eyes shut. I had no time to waste. With my hands, I found her purse. I opened my eyes, and opened the purse. It was full of gimcracks and written information in the form of a stuffed wallet. All I learned was that she carried a great deal of money, but it was her reaction to my search that I wanted most.

"He's in my wallet!" she cried in the living room. She was at the bedroom door immediately. "Stay out of my personal possessions!" she blazed.

I nodded gratefully. "Thank you very much, dear. You've been an unfailing help. Now—what's in your wallet that could give you away?" I thumbed through the leaves of a ring-bound insert. "Ah. These would be photographs." Like the television picture, they were flat and colorless under their protective celluloid.

She tried to snatch them, and I slapped her hand. Carefully I studied the pictures.

Alicia and Champley on the steps of an elaborate home. Alicia and Champley in a car, she at the wheel. Nothing else of interest, unless one counted a dozen poses of Alicia in her beauty-contest winning days.

I pursed my lips, and turned toward her. Something caught the corner of my eye. It was a glassy color picture, almost life-sized, of a dark, narrow-faced man. It hung from the back of the bedroom door, and moved.

"Who's that?" I asked sharply.

"That?" She laughed. "Why, that's a mirror. That's *you*, Will!"

"The Devil it is!" I snapped. Why do they think the blind don't know what they look like? Those pathetic scenes in the novels—the blinking eyes, fresh out from under the bandages; the upheld hand mirror; the wondering gasp: 'Is—is that *me*?' Claptrap. Move the muscles of a face for forty years—feel the flesh twist—shave it, touch it . . . what, in Heaven's name, do they think a blind man would have most immediately available for his study of the world, if not his own body? Color, no. Texture, shape diagrammatic configuration, *yes*. At the very least, no one could ever foist a total stranger on . . .

I stopped dead still and touched my face. And it wasn't mine. I thought of the photographs. Alicia and *Champley*?

"*Champley!*" I flung the wallet into the living room. I thrust Alicia out of the way. Champley was standing just inside the living room, a hypodermic syringe waiting in his hand. I knocked it aside and closed my hands on his throat. "What did you do?" I asked calmly, calmly increasing the pressure. "How did we trade bodies?"

He could not answer, and pawed feebly at my arms. After a little while, I found myself able to let him go. I pushed him into a chair.

"Well," I said, "now I know what it profits Alicia." Alicia, dabbing at her eyes, slumped on the arm of his chair and stroked his neck.

I marched back and forth across the room, taking stock. "All right. The monster comes out from behind that secret door. He has no other escape, unless it's down a drop great enough to kill or seriously injure him. I say escape because he has an urgent desire but cannot as yet fulfill it. Q.E.D., you've got him caged in there. But he's working loose, and you don't dare go near him to secure him once more. All right. He comes out, he rolls into this room. What does he find? Does he find a blind stranger? No, he finds Doctor Champley. He eats me, and you and Alicia live happily ever after. Good. So far, there's logic.

"More logic: you need a perfectly functioning Doctor Champley. You want Alicia. Both of you want my money. *Ergo*: You switch bodies with me, while ostensibly restoring my sight. You *do* restore my sight, because you're having no trouble seeing out of my eyes. Very good. Everybody's problem is solved. You perform these two complicated operations inside of an hour. Hold. Alicia *says* you do it inside an hour. No matter. You perform these complicated operations. That's marvelous enough, considering you had to be operating on yourself part of the time. How'd you do it—brain transplant? Good trick. Transmigration of souls? Just as good, but more complicated. Settle for brain transplant. Dandy trick. Impossible. How did you operate on yourself? You trusted another doctor? Faugh! You wouldn't trust your own mother.

"All right. You can do two impossible things before breakfast. I don't believe a word of it. No. You've got an automatic surgical machine, or machines. No such thing exists. No operative technique exists which would leave you and me walking around normally inside of a week, without a scar or a twinge. You're the one with the new eyes, and you're holding up perfectly. You've got hold of some fantastic medical techniques Johns Hopkins never heard of. Where'd you get 'em? What about you is different from every other living soul? *You've* met and offended a monster. Monster. Backtrack that.

Alien. Alien being from some other world. Some other world with superior science. All right.

"All right, that's the source of your skill. Why does the monster hate you? Why did he give you *medical* skills? How did you get him caged in here?"

I stopped and drove my fist into my open palm. "Done!" I swung toward Champley and pointed my finger between his eyes. "The alien was sick. He probably crashed. He was injured, and told you how to help him. You agreed to patch him up, but you ran out on him instead, and started in on becoming a Park Avenue surgeon. Now you're fat and frightened. The monster's going to get you. What to do? You find a substitute for yourself—and I'm the patsy. Prove me wrong."

Champley's mouth opened. "I—"

"Prove me wrong!"

Champley shook his head. "No . . ." he said huskily. "Y'r right."

"And what are you going to do about it?" Alicia demanded triumphantly. "Are you going to force Louis to re-transplant?" She laughed. "You *can't* do it. You can kill him, you can beat him—nothing you can do to him can possibly be as bad as what a loathsome thing like that beast would do to him. You can't even *buy* your way out. You can't *think* your way out. No one but Louis can set up the surgical machine, and he would sooner die. But—kill him and what have you gained?"

"Kill him? Kill my own body? That wouldn't be my kind of thinking, Alicia. Let's try another tack."

"You can try all you want to. You're boxed in, Will."

"I doubt it. No part of this plan has gone right for you. I see no reason why the rest of it should."

"None of the other parts were important."

"I was referring to the general level of intelligence displayed."

"I hope you don't wonder why I'd be glad to get rid of you."

"In the most horrible way you could conjure up. Yes." I smiled. "I never wonder about anything, Alicia. I find out."

There was a perceptible creaking from the back of the

cottage. Something quite large was pressing against the kitchen wall.

"What happens if I run for it?" I said thoughtfully. "No. That's no good. One, I'd be on foot and ignorant. You'd have a car to head me off. Two, it would take me some time to establish my identity, and some time longer before I dared tell anyone I had a monster locked up in a summer cottage. Three, Champley might be able to pass for me, with your coaching. Most important, that's a sloppy approach to the problem. The problem's here, and we're all here. Let's get at it."

"Never make it," Champley said, rubbing his throat. "You're good as dead. And you're welcome."

I sat down. "You two don't count. Only the situation gives you your power. All right, change the situation. Disarm you. Make friends with the alien."

"Wish you luck," Champley said. "He's been back there for eight years. He was in agony when he crawled in, and he's been in agony ever since. He hasn't eaten. He hasn't rested. He's been in there, while I waited for him to die, and I wouldn't be surprised if the only thing that keeps him alive is hate."

His voice went up in trembling hysteria, badly controlled. "He won't *die*! I waited. I waited, and he didn't die. He only grew more desperate. You can hear him. He doesn't care anymore how much he hurts himself. He won't die until he gets to me." Then he remembered what he'd done to me, and bared his teeth in joy. It must have been an especially virulent degree of fear that had been haunting him.

"Let's think about this monster," I said. "Monster's what you call him. Let's try calling him an alien. Stranger in a strange land. Hurt. Lost his transportation—his spaceship, his whatd'youcallit, whatever he uses—or he'd limp home. All right. He's trapped, and hurt. Eight years? He's tough. But he can't function well. Along comes a native. What were you, Champley—medical student? Mail-order college quack? Somebody who might help. He establishes communication.

"Ah. *How*, Champley? How did you talk to each other?"

"Why don't you try torturing me to find out?"

"Umn. Might. Later. Let's see if I can work around you. . . . It wasn't television. That's one-way. Does he ordinarily talk in electromagnetic frequencies? When he's among his own kind? Interesting. All I need is a microphone and a transmitter, then. None available. Out. All right. How did *you* talk to him. What kind of wig-wag system'd you use? Telepathy? No. Or this plan of yours would have collapsed a-borning."

I looked up at Champley. "No—it *couldn't* be: plain English speech? This whole substitution would never stand up . . . or, wait, yes it would. Monster comes out, propelled by years of hatred. Sees Champley—sees me. Champley says: 'Wait! I'm really William Schaeffer.' Does the monster listen? Does it stop? Would I?

"Plain English speech does it, Champley. All I have to do is go in the kitchen and talk to it while it's still trapped."

Champley reached into his pocket and brought out a flat, glittering blued thing. "All right, Schaeffer. That did it," he said. He pointed it at my knee, and I realized it was a gun. When he fired it, there was a loud noise, and my thigh wrenched as though a swinging girder had jabbed it. I cupped it in my hands and stared at it, grinding my lips between my teeth.

"Does it hurt, Will?" Alicia murmured.

"Don't worry," Champley told her. "It hurts. Now—Schaeffer; are you going to sit still and do what I tell you, or are you going to try to talk to the monster? I can cripple your other leg. And then your arms. I can leave you helpless on that bed. I suppose I could even break your spine. All I have to do is bandage you up, put new clothes on you over the bandages, and I don't think the monster'll stop to inspect you too closely."

There was a wet look to his and Alicia's faces. That would be perspiration, I thought.

Champley said: "I don't *like* you, Schaeffer. You're too slippery. Too quick. I'm not as smart as you are. The only thing I can do is to be completely ruthless."

"That's not reserved for the exclusive use of the stupid," I said.

He licked his lips. "I don't want to break you up, Schaeffer. If possible, I want you moving when the monster comes out." He looked at me with a narrow-eyed smile. "I'd think you'd prefer to have a chance to run for it."

"Hobble for it," Alicia said.

"Crawl for it. Yes," I said, "no doubt that would be the ordinary man's preference. Perhaps it's mine."

"Quit it!" Champley cried. "I'm the man with the gun. Quit trying to take the initiative away from me! Now—be reasonable, damn you! You sit quiet and stop trying to wiggle out of this, and maybe you'll be in shape to get away from it when it comes out."

"I will make no further moves toward contacting the alien," I said.

He relaxed. "Good. Now—roll up the leg of your pants. Alicia, get a compress out of my bag. We can't have him bleeding to death."

"He'll grab me if I go over to him!" Alicia cried.

"I'll have the gun on him!" Champley said angrily. "He won't try anything!"

"He'll try anything!" Alicia answered back.

"Maybe he will and maybe he won't," Champley cried. "Would you rather have the monster grab *me*? Now, *do what you're told*!"

"Don't *shout* at me!"

"All right," Champley said in a hard voice, seething with temper. "I'll just point the gun at you. That's better than shouting."

Something massive rolled against the kitchen wall, and the house trembled.

"Just you remember something!" Alicia shouted at Champley. "Just you remember this plan of yours doesn't work out at all without me! Even if you get away from the monster, you're *nothing* without me!"

"By God, I might just try it and see if you're right about that or not!"

"Champley. Alicia," I said. I took my hands away from my thigh and watched the blood spurt. It was pumping out with considerable force. That would be an arterial flow, I thought, raising my eyes and looking at them calmly.

"My God!" Alicia whispered.

"Get that compress," Champley said. "Get it quick! He's doing that *deliberately*!"

They hurried through the business of compressing my leg. It would have been absolutely stupid to take physical action against them. They weren't my antagonists.

The house shook again. Something broke in the kitchen wall with a loud crack.

Champley wiped his face. Alicia jumped up and stood erect. "I'm getting out of here. I'm going to wait out in the car."

"You stay here and finish tying up that compress! And when you're through with that, you're going to wipe up the rug and get new pants on Schaeffer."

"Shut up, the two of you," I said. I reached down and tied the bandage. Getting to my feet, I started across the room.

"Sit *down*, Schaeffer!" Champley shouted.

"I'm going into the bedroom to change my trousers. I'm not going to try to contact the alien. You and Alicia had better get busy at getting the blood off the floor." I made my clumsy way into the bedroom, hoping I had not overestimated the amount of blood I could spare and still continue to function normally. If they were going to keep on quarreling. I needed a quiet place to think. They were irritating me with their pettiness.

The monster had cut into the television circuits. He hadn't done it with apparatus. If he'd had any sort of machinery in there with him, he would long ago have converted it into a cutting tool. He would not be smashing himself bodily against that wall. Not in his condition. No matter how wrought-up he was. All right, he could use electromagnetics without apparatus. That was an extra-normal ability he had.

One. If it was his only one, why did he waste that one possible trump card on a melodramatic gesture? Was he a fool? If he was a fool, I could either handle him on the spur of the moment or else no logical plan would work against him. Stop planning?

No. Assume he knows what he's doing. Assume more than one difference between him and a human being. Keep planning.

What kind of difference? Where's a pipeline into his brain? What do I use to get a hold on him?

Why was he breaking out exactly now? His fury was reaching a climax, but how had he known Champley was in the cottage at just this time?

Had he heard Champley's—my—voice?

I'd been in the cottage a week. Why was he moving now, and only now. I hadn't heard *him* before today. Were his ears sharper than mine?

Was my voice Champley's?

No. No, by God. My brain used vocal cords in a different way from Champley's. Champley and I were about of a size, and our voices roughly in the same range, but Champley's vocal cords couldn't possibly be identical in length and thickness with mine.

"Alicia!"

"What?" she asked shrilly from the other room.

"Nothing." I fastened the belt of the fresh pair of trousers. It was much more my voice than it was Champley's. It wasn't mine, but close enough to it to fool me through gauze wrapped carefully over my eyes and ears.

The alien couldn't have recognized it. He had some other way of knowing. . . .

The cottage shook. I stepped quickly out into the living room.

The kitchen wall broke down. There was a lurch, a tearing of nails out of wood, and something remorseless came rolling into the living room.

Alicia screamed, and Champley cried: "There he is—over there—that's Champley."

The alien made straight for Champley, took him, reached out, and took Alicia. They hung in the air.

"I have a business proposition to make," I said to the alien.

From somewhere on itself, the alien said: "Let's hear it."

Alicia drove the car, with Champley lolling beside her, his mouth slack and wet. The alien sat on the back seat beside me, covered by a blanket like a bundle of old clothes. From time to time, the alien reached out with part of itself and stroked Champley's neck. Whenever he did, Champley burst into tears.

"Oh, God," Alicia mumbled to herself all the way into New York. "Oh, God, it's all edges and angles and thorns. All black and all slick and all rolling."

"We're agreed, then," I said to the alien. "As soon as Champley and I have re-exchanged bodies, I will use the machine to heal you. Then my subsidiary corporations will begin construction of a new interstellar vessel for you. In return, you will pass to us as much scientific knowledge as we are capable of encompassing."

"Agreed," the alien said from under his covering. "You're much more satisfying to deal with than that other one."

"I should have known you'd recognize Champley no matter what disguise he was wearing."

"Recognize? Champley? I thought all you people were named Champley."

"No," I said slowly, "I, for instance, am William Schaeffer."

"Interesting," the alien said. "Well. Now I have to revise my warning. I like you, but that's beside the point. We're engaged in business. I have to say that if you betray me, I will get you, William Schaeffer. You understand that?"

"It's the best practical basis for doing business. Clear-cut."

"Yes. We're both practical men," the alien said. "I thought Champley was the best I could do, and took the chance. It's a shame I can't read minds, or I wouldn't have made the mistake. But I can literally see the presence of practicality, like a glow shining around a man's mind."

"You can," I said.

"Certainly," the alien told me. "I'm amazed at the difference in degree between you and Champley. It's the only worthwhile measure of intelligence. And as you said, practicality is the only worthwhile rule of conduct. In any environment, it's mandatory always to deal with the most practical creature and discard the others before they can muddle the picture. The ability to sense practicality directly is an invaluable survival trait. It has raised my people to the heights. It is what separates us from the animals. It is the test of humanity."

The alien touched me gently with part of himself. I felt nothing that would make me laugh or cry. It was simply a contact between two equals. He said, "That's why I took steps to remove Champley and that other person from any effective interference between us. I could instantly sense a brother in you."

And so we rode into New York City. So I became William Schaeffer again. And now there is an alien race in the stars which is today a friend of Mankind.

DREAM OF VICTORY

CHAPTER I

FUOSS CRACKED HIS knuckles and pushed the empty glass across the bar. He took a pull on his cigarette, driving the smoke into his lungs as hard as he could. He exhaled a doughnut-shaped cloud that broke against the bartender's stomach.

"Want another one, Mister?" the bartender asked.

Fuoss bit down hard, enjoying the pressure on his teeth. "I'll take one."

The bartender picked up the glass. "I don't think she's coming in tonight."

"Who?"

"Carol. It's a little late for her to be in."

"Carol who?"

"You kidding, Mister?"

Fuoss pushed the stub of his cigarette into an ashtray, took out another one and waited for it to light. "I never knew a

Carol in my life. You trying to sell me on a friend named Carol?"

"You know how many of these you've had, Mister?" The bartender held the glass up.

Fuoss bit down again. "You keeping tab?"

"Sure I am. I was just wondering if you knew." The bartender poured a finger of lemon juice into his mixer. "You're an android, aren't you?"

"What's that got to do with it?" Fuoss cracked his knuckles in the opposite direction.

The bartender added gin. "Carol's human. Grew up on the block. I remember the first time she came in here, with this look on her face daring me to say she wasn't old enough." The bartender, who was a bulky man, was apparently used to having globules of sweat tremble on his forehead. "Carol's human," he repeated, without raising his glance from the mixer.

Fuoss's stool clattered on the floor.

The bartender looked up. The door shut loudly. The bartender ducked under the bar and ran to the door. He looked through the glass but couldn't see anything, so he opened the door and stuck his head outside. A sound of footsteps came from down the street, but the street lamp in front of the bar cut off his vision.

The bartender quirked his mouth up at the corners. He went back inside the bar, set the stool up, and drank the Tom Collins himself.

In sleep, the conscious mind—that cohabitant collection of mis-directed clockwork—is quiescent, and the dramatic subconscious is free of its restraints.

Seven-thirty.

Fuoss's day began. Usually, the shift from subconsciousness back to conscious thought was so precise that he was able to believe that he never dreamt, but this morning the fatigue of the previous day's unusually hard work held nim on the borderline.

Seven-thirty, then, in the clock's modulated voice, and

Fuoss let the end of a snore trickle out of his nostrils, closed his mouth, and scratched a buttock, but was not yet completely awake.

Seven-thirty and a half. Recall the length and complexity of the dream that comes between the first alarm and the subsequent feel of the bedside carpeting under your feet as you gather your pajama bottom back up to your waist. Mohammed knocked a glass from a table, bent, caught it, and dreamed a lifetime in the interval.

Fuoss pushed the clock's cutoff and walked to the bathroom, skirting his wife's bed. He shaved and showered, walking back into the bedroom with his pajamas over his arm. He went to the night table between the twin beds, picked up a cigarette, then sat down on his bed instead of taking fresh underwear out of the bureau and dressing.

"Stac?"

His wife had awakened. She turned her head and looked at him, raising a hand to brush the hair out of her eyes. "You're not getting dressed. What's the matter?"

Fuoss widened his eyes and relaxed them, trying to come fully awake. "I don't know," he said. "I had this dream just before I woke, and I'll be damned if I can remember it. Guess I just sat down for a minute, trying to remember it."

"Is that all?" Lisa smiled. "Why let a dream bother you?" She stretched her arms at her sides, bending them upward at the elbows. "Kiss me good morning."

Fuoss smiled, threw the cigarette into an ashtray, and bent over the bed. "Does sound silly, doesn't it? Can't get the idea out of my head that it's important, though."

Lisa raised her lips. Her swollen eyes and mouth were crusted at the corners. Fuoss kissed her absently.

"Stac! What the devil's the matter with you this morning?"

Fuoss shook his head. "I don't know. It's that damned dream. I haven't felt right since I woke up. Can't pin it down."

Lisa frowned. "Whatever it was, I don't like it. From the way you kissed me, you'd think it was about another woman."

Fuoss felt a jab of guilt. He got up from Lisa's bed and

walked over to the bureau. The taste of Lisa's unwashed mouth was on his lips, and he yanked at the top drawer.

"If I knew I wouldn't be bothered about it, would I?" He dressed rapidly. "Do I have to kiss you like Don Juan every morning?" He went to the night table and picked up his watch and keys. "Haven't got time for breakfast, now. I hope Brownfield's wife finally had her kid, so Tom can get back to the office. I'm getting sick of doing his work overtime without getting paid for it."

Lisa made an impatient sound, got up and walked toward the bathroom. She slept naked. Fuoss watched her.

"Arms and legs," he said. "Two of each, perfectly molded, attached with correct smoothness, and equally smoothly articulated and muscled. Breasts and hips—also two of each—and superbly useless for anything but play. All this equipment joined to a sculptured torso, and the entire work of the designer's art surmounted by a face with just enough deliberate irregularities to make it appealing."

Lisa turned, a half-frightened look on her face. "What did you say?"

Fuoss smiled with restrained bitterness. "That was just Culture S, Table C Fuoss reading specification on Culture L, Table S ditto. My wife, by the grace of Section IV, Paragraph 12 of the Humanoids Act of 1973, and the General Aniline Company, Humanoids Division. Good morning, Mrs. Mannikin—"

Whatever it was that had been fermenting in him suddenly came to a head. "Why the hell don't you buy a hairnet?" he said, and slammed the bedroom door behind him.

Fuoss stepped out of the Up chute into the office a few minutes before nine. He went to his desk and sat down, staring at the In basket which the file clerks had already filled with folders and correspondence. He ran a thumb along the edge of a batch of files.

Blue Tabs. McMillin. First Brownfield's stuff and now McMillin's, too. There wasn't anything wrong with Mac's wife. Why should he be doing part of his stuff?

He wiped his forearm over his eyes. He'd tried to explain

this morning's outburst to himself during the drive to the office. It couldn't be the dream. He was tired. Work had been piling up on his desk during the past month, and he'd had to do overtime. Brownfield had been out lately, with his wife's pregnancy developing complications at term. That meant more work to be done. More reading, more dictation, more interviews. His nerves were strained.

He remembered some of the other jobs he'd worked at. Doing rewrites for the *Times*, for instance. He'd liked it, been good at it. He'd saved enough from that so the extra money he'd picked up free-lancing had paid for the destruction and replacement of the unmatured remainder of Lisa's culture. At that time, the thought of being married to a true individual had seemed important.

After the newspaper business got a little tight, he'd tried his hand at managing a chain store, and when that petered out he'd done any number of other things, until he'd finally landed this insurance claim adjusting job. Come to think of it, he'd held a lot of jobs.

Guess I'm the restless type, he decided.

". . . and thank you for your kind cooperation," he dictated an hour later. "Rush that out, will you, Ruthie?"

He looked up from the file and saw Brownfield come in.

"Thank God!" he said. Brownfield was carrying a box of cigars and wearing the smile of a new father. "Look who's here."

"Why, it's Mr. Brownfield! He called this morning and said he might be in," the stenographer said.

But they figured I might as well do his work anyway, huh? Fuoss thought. "What's the news on his wife?" he asked.

"Oh, she's fine. They had a baby boy." Ruth smiled enviously.

Brownfield came across the office to his desk. Fuoss got up. "Well, hell, Tom, congratulations!" he said, slapping Brownfield on the back. "Boy, huh? Bet he looks like his mother. Most boys do, I hear."

"Little early to tell yet, Stac," Brownfield said happily. "Might be, though. He's got blue eyes like Marion."

"Well, all babies have blue eyes at first," Fuoss said. The thought struck him that young Brownfield probably resembled nothing so much as he did a slightly boiled marmoset.

"All babies do?" Brownfield said. "I didn't know that. How come you did?"

Meaning "What does an android know about children," huh? You smug son of a bitch. "Don't know. Must have read it somewhere, I guess," he said.

"Guess so. Have a cigar?"

"Thanks. Say, these are good."

"Nothing but the best for the first-born, I always say."

Fuoss hid a grimace. "What're you going to call him, Tom—Junior?" he asked unnecessarily.

"What else? Have to carry on the family names, you know."

In a pig's left nostril, I know!

Brownfield looked over his desk. "Looks like all my work's been done for me while I was gone. You do it?"

"Uh-huh."

"Well, boy, I owe you a drink, don't I? What say we drop in some place after work? I sure appreciate you doing this for me."

Why not?

"Sure. I'll see you at five."

"Sure thing." Brownfield walked away, the open box of cigars in his hand.

Fuoss threw the cigar into the back of his desk drawer and picked up another file.

Carol had short, dusty-black hair. Her blue eyes were wide. They were accented by sweeping brows and outlined by coal-black lashes. Her nose was short, flat, turned up at the end. Her lips were small and thin. They twisted nervously whenever she forgot to control them. Her face was round, suntanned, and slightly flat.

Fuoss waved at the waitress and silently pointed to the three empty glasses. The girl put the glasses on her tray and moved off.

Brownfield shifted awkwardly in his chair. "I've got to go home, Stac," he said petulantly. "It's getting late. I've got to call the hospital and talk to my wife."

Fuoss looked at him from under his lowered eyebrows, his eyes a dark mud color. "You can call her from here."

"I'm hungry, too. I've got to go home and eat."

"You can order a sandwich here, you know." Fuoss took a pack of cigarettes out of his shirt pocket and held it out to Carol.

"Light it for me, will you?" she said.

Fuoss grinned. He put two cigarettes in his mouth until they lit, and handed one over. "Tommie boy, here, gave me a cigar today," he said. "Good cigar. Too bad I hate cigars." He turned to Brownfield, smiling. "Don't get me wrong, Tommie. You're a hell of a good Joe. I just don't like cigars." He leaned across the table and laid his hand on Carol's arm.

"Tommie sure did me a big favor today," he said emphatically. "He brought me in here, didn't he? Introduced me to one of the really nicest people I ever met. Even if I don't like cigars. Was that Tommie's fault? Good cigar. Did his best." He laughed. "Sure did his best. Mr. Brownfield has fathered a son. Ever hear of a better best than that?"

Carol shook her head. "Never did. That's really something."

Brownfield pushed his chair back. "I've got to go."

Fuoss narrowed his eyes and stared at him. He looked at Carol with a sidewise swing of his eyes and then looked back at Brownfield. "All right. 'F I was you I'd be celebrating the blessed event, but I guess you know what you're doing. Thanks for the drink. And thanks for introducing me to Carol. Goodbye."

Brownfield grinned uncomfortably and raised his hand awkwardly. "I'll see you." He turned his awkward smile in Carol's direction. "I'll see you, too."

"Won't wifey mind?" Carol answered, puffing on the cigarette. "It's been fun and all that, but you're a proud papa now."

Brownfield put his hand on the back of his chair and

opened his mouth, but closed it again and then said something else instead: "Yeah. I guess so. I—I'll see you." He turned and walked out.

Carol broke into a laugh. "Ever see an expression like that on anybody's face before?"

Fuoss guffawed. "Not once. Never." The waitress had brought three fresh drinks, and he picked up Brownfield's. "Brownie's a good guy, though. Never thought a bird like him knew about a place like this. Damnedest thing."

"The place isn't really much. It's too quiet, usually. I like it to rest up in until the bigger places open."

Fuoss looked around and nodded. "Yeah, come to think of it, you're right. The place would be dead if I hadn't run into you. I guess it's the company that gives any place its atmosphere."

He finished Brownfield's drink and started on his own. "Damnedest thing, us just walking in here and finding you."

Carol smiled. "Oh, I'm usually in here. It's awfully dull, usually."

Fuoss nodded. "Come to think of it," he said abruptly, "Brownie was right. It is time to eat. You hungry?"

Carol nodded, wrinkling her nose. "Uh-huh."

"Okay. Order something. You know the food in here. Order for both of us."

"Oh, the food stinks in this place. Tell you what . . ." Carol smiled, dimpling sweetly. "Why don't we go up to my place? I'll cook something up for us and we can go out someplace later. How's that?"

Fuoss's eyes glittered. "Sounds good," he said, and waved to the waitress for their check.

There was no point to going all the way back to the carport to pick up Fuoss's Buick, so they took a cab to Carol's apartment. Fuoss helped her out of the cab and held her coat while she unlocked the door.

She opened the door and swayed against him. "Whew! I didn't know I was that high," she murmured. She laughed, a low chuckling laugh and leaned forward.

“ ’S all right,” Fuoss said. “ ’S all right. We’ll be okay when we get some food down.”

“Sure we will,” Carol said, and laughed again. “Mix yourself a drink while I go find the kitchen.”

Fuoss was recording impressions on his senses. There were a lot of them. They wheeled by; sight, hearing, smell, taste, feel, all reeling by. He had no means of slowing them down or cutting them off, so he simply recorded, letting them run into his mental tape recorder, not analyzing, not examining, just letting them spin, stopping once in a while to drive his fingernails into his forearm when the fog became too pervasive.

Slap! His head recoiled. *Slap!* Other direction. He was leaning against the flextile bathroom wall, facing the mirror. He slapped himself again. And again, trying to drive some of the fuzz out from around his senses. The air was tight, squeezing against him from all directions, compressing.

There was just too much of it. Too much going on, going by. He opened his eyes and the spinning stopped. No, not quite. But it did slow down considerably.

Carol’s arm was around his neck. “Hi,” she said, wrinkling her nose.

“Hi.” He pouted a smile in return.

“I don’t think we’re going out after supper.” She giggled.

“Why not?”

“It’s two o’clock in the morning and we haven’t had supper yet.”

Fuoss looked down at a coffee table covered with bottles. Most of them had been sampled. “Well, let’s eat, then.” He was having real trouble focussing his eyes.

Carol put her other arm round his neck. “In a minute, honey. Let’s have one more drink. We haven’t tried the Cherry Heering yet.” She nuzzled his ear.

Fuoss stifled a belch. “All right.”

Just before morning he had the dream again.

He thrashed out in the night, twisting the sheet around his

legs and bringing a sleepy protest from Carol. He kicked, but the sheet held. He was soaking in sweat.

He had no clear image of the woman. She remained disembodied. Discarnate, but woman incarnate. He knew only that she was human, and this knowledge brought him a sense of triumph, of victory. He was victorious, glorious.

She came from blackness, and it was into blackness that he went for her.

He rolled and jerked on the bed. Time whinnied by like a silver beast.

The woman was gone, hidden in blackness. His feet moved spasmodically against the sheets.

The blackness parted and the woman returned. There was with her—

His subconscious recoiled. He cried out.

"Stac!"

The infant turned from his mother's breast and stretched out his hands. "Father!"

"Wake up, Stac! Goddam it, *wake up*!" Carol pounded his shoulder. "Wake up, will you, for Christ's sake! You're bawling like a baby."

Fuoss opened his eyes and looked up into the darkness. He reached out for Woman.

Fuoss stayed behind a pillar, out of sight of the hundreds of arriving commuters, until his car was driven down the ramp. Then he scrambled inside and drove out of the exit as rapidly as possible. He swung into the Uptown lane and relaxed for the first time since stepping out of the cab at the carport.

A dose of B-1 had calmed his stomach, but his head was still feverish. His hands had a tendency to shake. When he paid his toll at the bridge, he almost dropped the coin. He drove jerkily, tramping down on the accelerator and letting up too fast on the brake.

Despite this, there was a smile of satisfaction on his face.

Lisa met him at the door. "Tal's here," she said.

"The old family legal advisor, huh? Going to get a divorce

before you even hear my side of the story?" Fuoss twisted his mouth.

Lisa smiled coldly. "If you're going to go tom-catting, I can't stop you, but at least get the purr out of your voice when you come back. Tal called up early this morning—wanted to see you. When I told him you weren't in, he came over to wait for you."

"Uh-huh. The office call?"

"Yes. I had to tell them you were sick. I don't think they believed me."

Fuoss grinned sourly. "Not with Brownie running around telling them what a bad boy I've been." He shrugged. "Tal in the living room? I'll go in and talk to him."

He brushed his lips across Lisa's cheek. "Fix me some breakfast, will you, honey?"

Tal Cummins, like most androids, was the next thing to a chain smoker. He opened a gold case as Fuoss came in and threw him a cigarette without asking.

"How are you, Stac?"

Fuoss sat down opposite him. "Fair. What's up?"

Cummins waited until his cigarette had a good light. His black hair had fashionable gray strands in it. His face was lean and aristocratic. His manner matched them. He had bought the hair and face to replace the ordinary undistinguished android features, but the manner had taken a number of years to cultivate. Only with another android did he fail to rise, murmur a greeting, and offer his cigarette case with polite urbanity. "How's your job coming along?" he finally asked.

"Hell of a question after two years."

Cummins tapped his cigarette and watched the ash drift into a tray. "Doing a lot of overtime lately, are you?"

"Sure."

"Getting paid for it?"

"Supper money. Executives don't draw overtime—you know that."

Cummins snorted. "Ever hear of the Junior Executives

Union? Don't tell me—the answer's no. It's a part of the dead and glorious Prewar past. The companies beat it by putting everybody from file clerks on up on the private payroll. Bingo, they were ineligible for unionization."

"And I'm that kind of an executive, huh?"

"You're in good company." Cummins let some more ash fall. "How about the other fellows in your office? They do a lot of extra work?"

"Not much. I sort of take care of about everything around here."

"I'll bet you do. How's your production record? Handle more cases than anybody else in the office, don't you? Even with the extra work, I mean."

"Sure. It's pretty easy work."

"Getting steady raises, are you?"

"Well—times are a little rough in the insurance game. They promised me one pretty soon, though." Fuoss ran a hand through his hair. "What's all this getting at?"

Cummins doused his cigarette. "Did it ever strike you that you were being put upon, old chum? Don't you think it's kind of funny that a guy with your ability has held so many jobs?"

Fuoss grunted. "Maybe. I was thinking about it yesterday, as a matter of fact." Tal Cummins is a hell of a nice guy, but I'd like him better if he didn't talk in circles. He shifted his feet.

Cummins smiled thinly. "I'll get to the point in a minute."

"Mind reader?" Fuoss growled.

"Lawyer." Cummins let himself smile for a minute more, wasted a little time on a new cigarette, then leaned forward. "Stac, I'll bet you anything you'd care to risk that you'll lose your job within the month."

"Why?"

"May I acquaint you with a little history?"

"If it's got anything to do with me. But cut it short."

"History is never short, my boy." Cummins kicked the end of his cigarette with his thumbnail. "History is extremely complicated, and we—" he gestured from Fuoss to himself, and included Lisa with a wave toward the kitchen, "are one of the prize complications.

"You've heard of the war. You have also heard of the extreme devastation and depopulation. I've done more than that. I've gone through books that describe a complicated civilization from its most revealing angle—its legal structure. I've also studied the 1960 census, and compared it with the emergency figures compiled in '68. Being an android, specializing in the cases covered by the Humanoids Act, I've also built up a better-than-average picture of what shape the humans were in when they finally dropped in their tracks in '67."

The sophisticated mask fell away. "Things were rugged, Stac. Seventy-five per cent of the civilized population was dead. Their technology was either completely wrecked or useless, because some fragment which remained operative depended on another part which hadn't. The humans were headed for the most colossal dark age since the Western Roman Empire collapsed.

"We were the answer. They took their soldier androids, did an extensive revamping and improving, and here we are. Or rather, there we were, because things are different now." The faintest trace of bitterness found an unaccustomed home on the bland features.

"Anyway," he went on, "what they needed in a hurry was a labor force. Not just a bunch of quasi-robots, but intelligent individuals, or near-individuals. who could handle anything a human could. The result was not only android pick-and-shovelers, but android technicians, android scientists, and android teachers. Even "—he smiled—" android lawyers."

"They did a good job. For all practical purposes, androids are duplicates of humanity. The main difference, of course, lies in the fact that androids cannot reproduce themselves by natural means. There, the humans knew they had a problem. If we were comparatively unintelligent, it wouldn't matter too much. But they gave us brains—and the potential for a nasty bundle of neuroses. They gave us android wives to take some of the sting off, but nobody's ever figured out a way to give us a substitute for parenthood. Adoption, unfortunately, is not the answer for the genuine article."

Fuoss looked at Cummins through a screening cloud of cigarette smoke. The lawyer was a smart cookie. Was he smart enough to be hinting around?

"But that's beside the point," Cummins said.

Fuoss relaxed.

"*That* problem is going to be solved as a by-product solution to a much larger problem," the lawyer continued. "In a way, your working overtime is a symptom of that same problem."

"How?"

"Look around you," Cummins said simply. "Any traces of the war left? Any poverty, hardship, devastation? You don't use matches on your cigarettes, you drive a two-hundred mph Buick with an automatic pilot, you never used an elevator in your life, and your alarm clock's been on voice for the last ten years. You, friend, are living in the technology of the late Twentieth Century. The fact that it's fifty years late is unimportant. Another thing—*this* civilization is truly worldwide. There are no 'backward' areas—the day of the ignorant savage gaping before the white man's magic is over."

"We did a good job," Fuoss said.

Cummins laughed, with no trace of humor. "Exactly. We worked ourselves right out of it."

"Now—wait a minute! You don't mean they're going to stop making androids."

"They have stopped."

"What! When? How come nobody knows about it?"

"Relax, Stac." Cummins waved him back into his chair. "There's nothing we can do about it. You'd be surprised how many people have tried." He smiled inscrutably. "I'm one of them, as a matter of fact. But there's more to worry about than that."

"Such as?"

"What's happening to you—and me. Haven't you figured it out yet? The human population's back up to normal. Nobody needs androids any more. They don't want to come right out and say so, and in many cases the humans themselves aren't deliberate in their actions. It's simply a question of an employer hiring humans rather than androids. After all, if you were a human employer, and two applicants, one human and the other android, showed up for the same job, which would you hire?"

"So I'm being eased out of my job?" Fuoss searched his pockets for a cigarette.

"Shows all the signs, doesn't it? Looks to me like they're trying to disgust you into resigning. They might also pick on some pretext—like you being out all night on a bat."

"That was a celebration with Tom Brownfield! He was with me!"

"All night?"

"All right—we split up about eight! So what?"

Cummins made another one of his soothing gestures. "Relax, boy. I'm not accusing you of selling anybody in slavery. I'm just saying your company might decide it was a beautiful opportunity. Insurance companies are pretty stuffy outfits, anyway, you know."

That was what Cummins said, but Fuoss could see the shrewd light in the lawyer's eyes. He'd let a little too much slip about last night. Worst of all, he'd protested too much. Well, there was nothing he could do about it now.

"So there won't be any more androids, huh?" Fuoss said.

"Correct. One of the obscurer subsections of the Humanoids Act covers the case. But why worry? One thing we androids have over the humans is a complete lack of interest in the succeeding generation."

"Don't be so Goddamned smug about it!"

Cummins raised his eyebrows. "Did I touch a sore spot?"

"Never mind what you touched. You've been spreading a lot of stuff around here this morning. I'm not ready to believe all of it. I particularly don't care about you prying into my married and personal life. Got me?"

Cummins got up, the urbane barrister once more. "Well, it seems I share Cassandra's popularity. Prophets without honor and all that. I'll be going."

"Good idea. I need some sleep."

"You do. And Stac . . ." Cummins paused on his way into the hall, "there's a law clerk's job open in my office when you need it."

"Go take a flying—"

"Goodbye."

Stac kept his eyes on Cummins until the lawyer had gone out of the door. Then he swung around and went into the kitchen. He stood just inside the door and looked at Lisa. His upper lip twitched.

"Breakfast's ready. Where's Tal?" Lisa said.

"Thanks. Tal's gone."

"What'd he want?"

Fuoss cut into a slice of ham. "Nothing much. Bunch of chatter, is all. Did he say anything to you about it?"

"No."

Fuoss looked up. Lisa was looking at him quietly.

"I was out with Brownie. His wife had a son and we were celebrating. That's all."

"All right, Stac." Lisa smiled. "Did you have that dream again?"

"Goddamn it!" Stac slammed his fist onto the tabletop. "Goddamn it to hell!"

CHAPTER II

Fuoss moved down the street. He stayed in the shadows and kept his footsteps light. He crossed the avenue and went into Carol's apartment house. He went into the lobby and pushed Carol's annunciator button.

A note, printed in Carol's handwriting, full of sweepingly crossed T's and curlicued S's, was thrown on the screen beside the button.

Hi, whoever—

Sorry—nobody's home. Don't know when I'll be back, but the lobby chairs are nice and cuddly if you want to wait. Or leave me a note.

See You.

Fuoss grimaced with satisfaction and turned the screen off. He went over to the chute, unlocked it, and rode to Carol's floor. He went down the hall to her apartment and let himself in.

Carol had left the lights on, as usual. He reached up to turn them off, then changed his mind. He went into the kitchen instead and took a can of beer. He removed the top and went into the bedroom, tilting his head back to let the beer slide down his throat.

The bedroom was a lot neater than he had expected it to be. The bedspread was folded over a chair and one of the vanity drawers was open, but the usual collection of washed but not yet ironed underthings was missing from the top of the bureau.

Fuoss put the beer can down on top of a table, went over to the closet and reached into a back corner. He pulled out his topcoat.

He put his hand in the left side pocket, fumbled around, grunted, tried the other pocket. He couldn't find anything in that one, either. He frowned and got to his hands and knees to search the closet floor. There was nothing there.

He swung the closet door angrily. A negligee that had slipped from its hanger kept it from closing completely. He pushed the negligee farther inside with his foot and slammed the door shut. He walked toward the bed, tangling his feet in the topcoat he had thrown to the floor. He kicked it up into reach and threw it on the bed. He moved over to the table, picked up his can of beer and drained it. He stood in front of the open bedroom window, bouncing the can in his hand.

He threw the can out and lay down on the bed. He propped his head up with two pillows so that he could watch the entrance to the apartment through the open bedroom door.

The office boy was about sixteen. He had pimples and an elaborate coiffure that had to be rebuilt by frequent recourse to a men's room washbasin and mirror. He liked to smirk.

"They wanna see you in the V.P.'s office, Mister Fuoss," he said.

"Thanks."

"Right away."

"Thanks."

"There's an awful lot of big shots in there."

"Scram."

"Huh?"

"Whip out of here, punk. If I'm getting the ax, I can at least stop acting like a human fountain pen. Now get going, before I wipe my nose with you." Fuoss stood up, and the boy backed out of the way.

"So Cummins was right," Fuoss muttered. He rummaged quickly through his desk, taking out his fountain pens and a few other items that belonged to him. He ran across Brownfield's cigar, grinned, and put it in his breast pocket.

He walked back between the rows of desks toward the Vice President's office. He had thought he'd be angry, or disappointed, perhaps, if Cummins' prediction actually came true. Instead, he discovered that he was feeling considerable relief. When he walked into the office, there was a slight smile at the corners of his mouth.

The office boy had been right. Aside from the division head, there was a complete representation of section supervisors. Brownfield sat in one corner.

"Good morning, Mr. Crofton, Mr. Mantell. Good morning, John, Harry, George," Fuoss said heartily. "Good morning, Brownie."

Crofton, the V.P., frowned. "Good morning, Fuoss. Sit down."

Fuoss moved into the indicated chair, crossed his legs and sat back. "What's up, W.C.?" One of the section heads snickered.

"I'd regard this occasion in a more serious light if I were you," Crofton said heavily.

Fuoss smiled. "It's a question of relative importance, I imagine," he said. He leaned forward. "Look, Mr. Crofton, let's cut this short. You're a busy man and I've got a new job to look for, so suppose I just have Ruthie run up a letter of resignation and we'll get this thing done right. Will any excuse do, or do you have some particular preference?"

There was an uncomfortable rustling among the section heads, but Crofton took it without any special reaction. "No. Almost anything will do. Make it effective next Wednesday. I'm sorry to see you go, Fuoss. On the other hand, I have no choice. You'll acquaint Mr. Brownfield with the cases you're handling currently." He extended a hand smilingly.

"Oh, I don't think I'll wait that long. Suppose I make it effective at five o'clock yesterday? And as for me acquainting Brownie with my current cases, that's hardly necessary, since most of them were his originally, anyway. Well, so long." He flipped a hand in salute and walked out.

Brownfield caught up with him in the cloakroom. "Say, Stac, I'm sorry this happened," he said, fumbling at Fuoss's sleeve. "It's just that when you didn't show up yesterday, somebody remembered that we went out together the night before and started asking questions."

"Sure, Brownie."

"I'm glad you're taking this so calmly," Brownie said, his face ineffectual.

"Sure. I'll see you around, huh, Brownie?" He put his jacket on, picked up his briefcase, and took the hand Brownfield extended. "Oh, yeah . . ." He reached into his breast pocket. "Have a cigar, Brownie."

Fuoss walked jauntily down the sidewalk toward the bar where he had met Carol. He picked up a paper at the corner newsstand, intending to check a few ads for luck. The sun was shining and a cool breeze came off the harbor.

He went into the bar and sat down. "Give me a gin and tonic, will you?" he said to the bartender and settled himself comfortably on the stool. His hands began to tremble, and he broke out in a sweat.

My God, what'm I going to do? I've got bills to pay, a wife to support. The rent's due pretty soon, and the tax instalment. What I've got in the bank won't carry me long. Where's it coming from?

He leaned forward and wrapped his fingers over the bar's molding. He began to tremble violently.

"You all right, buddy?" the bartender asked, setting a shot glass and a glass of quinine water in front of him.

"Fine. Just don't mix that drink, and bring me another shot of gin." He raised the shot glass to his mouth and sucked the gin out jerkily.

Carol came in at about four. Fuoss waved to her from the booth he'd spent the day in. She smiled and went over.

"Hi!"

"Hiya. Real higher. Pull up a drink and sit down," Fuoss said.

Carol laughed.

"Lost my job. Nobody loves androids any more. Rather have people. You rather have people?"

Carol shook her head. "That's too bad. *I* love androids." She moved her hand over, on top of his. "To hell with people."

Fuoss grinned happily. "You're people. But you're *nice* people. One of nicest people I know." He threw back his head and laughed.

"Say, you *are* packaged. You want to come over to my place and sleep it off?"

"Yeah. Yeah, I need it. Thanks, Carol. Thanks a lot. You're one of the best. No, really, you are." He pushed his way out of the booth and stood up weakly.

He had the dream again, that night.

Lisa's eyes were underscored by purple shadows. "Haven't we gone through this before, recently?"

Fuoss shut the door and dropped into a chair. "All right. Who'd you tell this time?"

Lisa's eyes widened with her failure to understand him.

Fuoss snorted. "Cut it out. I haven't known you for these years and not learned anything. Who?"

Lisa kept her eyes from his. "Tal."

"I thought so. Was he here again? To see me, of course."

"God, but you came back in a nasty mood!" Lisa clenched her fists, knuckles forward, woman-fashion.

"Long as I came back. That's all you've got to worry about. What'd you tell Cummins?"

"What do you mean what'd I tell him? I told him the truth."

"What's your version of 'the truth'?"

Lisa advanced toward him fiercely. "Stop it, Stac! I'm warning you—cut it out right now. I don't particularly give a damn if you spent the night in a hotel with some call girl, but don't come back in the morning and get nasty with me!"

Fuoss jumped out of his chair. Lisa's near-guess had come too close. He stood spraddle-legged in front of her, his arms shaking.

"Listen, baby," he said in a cold rage, "you're dead right. What I did last night is my own business." He bounced his palm off his chest. "At most, it's *our* business—yours and mine; not Tal Cummins's, not anybody else's. You've got a hell of a nerve standing there all housewifey, with that God-damned egg-sucking grin on your face, trying to bull me. And when I catch you lying"—he was breathing in short gasps—"you pull off the oldest defensive stunt in the world by flaring up at me!"

His head was pounding. He pulled a cigarette out of his pocket and stuck it in his mouth. "Listen, Lisa-so-ashamed of-being-an-android, Lisa-who-diddled-her-name-so-it-sounds-human, get me, *Lista*, and get me good! If it wasn't for me, you'd still be a sniveling shopgirl, and if it wasn't for me breaking my neck over a typewriter for five years, there'd be a carbon-copy of you on every block, and I'll bet my back teeth most of them wouldn't be too careful how they earned their keep, either. Just remember I set you up to a lifetime of Wednesday Bridge Clubs and Ladies Auxiliaries. Any time you decide you're going to get snotty with me, just run that over in your mind, and remember you're no better than a glorified animal cracker. I bought you, kid, lock, stock, and physiomolded backside. Now, clear out of my way and let me get some sleep."

"You bastard!" Lisa reached out an arm and clawed his face.

Fuoss ducked his head and pushed her away. He broke into short, high-pitched laughter. "Honey, that's one thing I *can't* be!" He turned around and walked toward the bedroom.

Lisa laughed too. "That's right. That's perfectly right. Just you remember that! You're nothing but a Goddamned android yourself."

Fuoss turned around. The blood had gone out of his face. He moved up on Lisa. "Watch yourself, baby. Be very careful what you say to me.

"In fact," he said slowly, "your troubles with me are over. Tal Cummins has clear title to you, at least as far as I'm concerned."

Carol was glad to have him move in with her. They spent the week-end in a drunken stupor and he had the dream again.

The personnel manager shook his head. "I'm sorry, Mr. Fuoss. We'd like to have a man of your experience with our organization, but we simply don't have any openings. Thank you for thinking of us, though, and we'll keep your application on file. I'll be sure to let you know if anything comes up."

"All right." Fuoss smiled and shook the man's hand. "Thanks, anyway."

"Certainly."

That night he and Carol got drunk together, and he had the dream again.

The next day a different personnel manager, for a company which would have paid five dollars a week less, was just as polite as the first.

An envelope from Tal Cummins' office had been delivered to him at Carol's apartment.

"How's it feel to be a co-respondent, hon?" Fuoss asked her.

Carol shrugged.

They got drunk, Fuoss took some sleeping pills, and they went to bed.

On the following morning, he went down to his bank and discovered that Lisa had drawn out exactly one-half of his account. He sold his car on the way down to the employment agency.

Fuoss noticed an item in a newspaper on the employment agency bench:

ANDROIDS URGED AS IDEAL FOR EXPLORATION OF SPACE

In a letter released today by the office of the Secretary of Defense, Tal Cummins, prominent android and well-known legal figure, urged the use of androids as crewmen in the projected attempt to put a manned rocket in an orbit around the Earth.

"Authorities agree," Cummins said in his letter, "that there is no sure way of knowing whether human beings can live in deep space under any conditions without actually making the attempt. I submit that androids provide an easy means of practical testing. Moreover, for this and similar projects, such as the proposed Moon rocket and the later expedition to Mars and Venus, specialized androids could be manufactured to meet special conditions, if it should prove that a humanoid organism cannot, for some reason, survive.

"Speaking for most androids, I can say that we would be glad to cooperate in any such program. Our satisfaction would lie in the knowledge that we had been of help in the greatest human undertaking since the dawn of civilization."

The office of the Secretary of Defense declined any official comment on the letter, but informed sources close to the Secretary admit that the proposal is being given serious consideration.

Fuoss's face was half-way between a scowl and a grin. "Half a loaf is better than none, eh, Cassandra?" he muttered. He re-read the story, which had drawn a two-column head on page two, and this time he scowled. He got up, found a nickel in his pocket and went to a pay phone in the corner. He dialed Cummins' number, talked his way past two secretaries, and was connected with the lawyer.

"Hello, Stac! How are you?" Cummins' voice and expression were as urbane as ever.

"Okay. How's Lisa?"

"I—don't know. I haven't seen her." The lawyer's tone was an almost successfully concealed mixture of anger and disappointment.

Fuoss bared his teeth. "If I had time, I'd laugh like hell." He would have, too. "I've been reading about you in the papers, Tal."

"You mean Project Spaceward?"

"Is that what they're calling it? Wouldn't Project Grab be more appropriate?"

"Just what do you mean by that?" Cummins was angry.

"That was a mighty clever piece of work, boy. If I were human, I'd fall for it myself. But I'm not, so I don't go for it." Fuoss chuckled. "Not that I give a damn. In fact, I think it's kind of a good joke on the humans. Boy oh boy, are they in for a shock when your satellite station androids 'prove' that humans can't survive the conditions. But that shock's not going to be anything, is it? Not compared to the one they'll get when they wake up to the fact that space belongs to the androids, and they had better be nice or they'll find themselves living on a second asteroid belt. I have to hand it to you, Cummins."

"All right, Stac. I won't try to kid you. That's exactly what I'm doing. Can you blame me? You, of all people. How many favors have the humans done you? They've fired you out of every job you ever held, and they're making it impossible for you to get another one. Tit for tat, Stac. They don't want us any more. All right—we'll give them Earth. But we'll take the rest of the universe for ourselves."

Fuoss shook his head. "Uh-huh. It might even happen. I hope so. But one thing stinks about this project, and that's you. You told me once that androids have no interest in their succeeding generation, remember? You were wrong. Whenever I see a young kid android, I try to do him all the favors I can. But as far as you're concerned, you were right. You look at life as a sort of Out-of-the-culture-dish, live a while,

Into-the-recovery-vat process. As far as you're concerned, android history began on your Awareness Day and will end with your death. So there's something in this for you, Cummins. There are mighty few drives left to an android. You've got the main one: power. Well, spin your little web. Dream your little dream. I hope you get away with it. Not because I like you. Because I hate humans more."

He laughed. "Just thought I'd let you know how I feel. So long, pal." He cut the connection and watched the lawyer's face dissolve on the screen.

That day he got a job, but he was carrying a bottle around with him by then, so he was paid off at three o'clock.

Carol wasn't there when he reached home, so he got drunk by himself. And that night he had the dream again.

One of the interviewers at the employment agency looked him right in the eye and said, in an impatient tone of voice, "Let's face it, Fuoss. You're not going to get anywhere with trying for white-collar work. Not anymore. There's no point in getting emotional about it; it's a plain fact. It's the way things are today, and you've got to accept it. Why don't you try something like construction work? Your pay'll be a lot bigger than you'll ever get in an office."

Fuoss did a mental run-down on his bank balance. "All right."

But the union just couldn't provide jobs for all its present members, much less take in a new one.

Tal Cummins had a guest appearance on a TV program, and spoke at some length about Project Spaceward. By the time he got to the end of it, Fuoss had gotten tired of waiting for Carol and gone to bed. He had the dream again.

Carol woke him up on Saturday morning and made breakfast.

After breakfast they sat down on the couch and smoked.

"Where were you these last two nights?" Fuoss asked.

"Out."

"Where?"

Carol turned her head and faced him. "Look, Stac, you're

a nice guy. I like you. But liking you hasn't got much to do with it. You're living here—that's O.K., so far, but you haven't got any strings on me."

Fuoss shrugged. "Okay—if that's how it is."

They spent a pretty miserable week-end.

Fuoss now took a job with a landscaping contractor out on Long Island. It paid a dollar and a half an hour, but it involved digging holes through fill that was well interlarded with brick halves, pieces of BX cable, folded lengths of thick tar paper, gravel and cinder block. His muscles weren't used to the job, but the worst strain was on his wrists, which took the shock of pick-swings that ended suddenly in some unseen obstacle. Nevertheless, he managed to last out the day without blistering his palms too badly.

When he rode back to the apartment that night, he felt better than he had in days.

Carol was home. He came in the door and she looked up. "Christ!" She stared at his clothes. "What've you been doing? Digging ditches?"

"That's right—just about, anyway. Digging holes for trees. You get your hands dirty, but you make money. Twelve bucks today." He grinned. He was feeling good.

Carol nodded. "Uh-huh. Twelve bucks. Go take a shower, will you?"

When he came out, she was waiting for him. She was walking around in haphazard circles, smoking a cigarette. "Sit down, will you, Stac?"

"Sure. What's cooking?"

"Look—today's the first of the month. Rent's due. You want to pay half of it?"

He frowned. "Christ, I'd like to, Carol. You know that. But I can't. I haven't got any money. I can give it to you in about two weeks."

"Yeah . . . maybe. And could you raise fifty-five more two weeks after that?"

"Hell, Carol, sure. Twelve bucks a day comes out to sixty a week."

"Before taxes, social security, unemployment insurance, transportation, lunches and cigarettes it does, yeah. Add laundry bills to that, too. What's more, this is August now. How much longer do you think landscaping's going to be open?"

"All right—so it's not the best job in the world!"

"I didn't say that. You should be able to make out pretty well with it, and they'll probably find you a winter job. Or else you can hole up on your unemployment checks. But not here, Stac. Not the way you're living." She flipped the cigarette into the sink.

"What're you trying to say?"

"I'm not trying—I'm saying. It's a matter of simple economics." She sat down beside him and put her hand on his knee. "Look, honey. I've been paying for your food the last two weeks. Some of the liquor we've mopped up you've bought, but most of it was here when you came. Up to now it hasn't cost you a dime to live here—or it wouldn't have, if you weren't a lush."

"Goddamn it! I am not a lush! I come home, we have a couple of drinks after supper, and then we start necking. Next thing we know, we're pie-eyed. But that doesn't make me a lush!" He realized that there were bigger things to argue over, but for some reason he kept pressing this point, as if concentrating on it would make the other problems disappear.

"Okay, honey." Carol stroked his hair. "Okay." She smiled. "You know, a doctor I knew once said that alcohol was an extreme form of sublimation. But I can't imagine what *you* would be sublimating." She grinned, and Fuoss grinned with her.

"Okay. I made a funny," Carol said. "That doesn't change anything. I can't afford to keep you, and you can't afford to stay. It's tough, but it's true." Impulsively, she put her arms around his neck. "Look, you ought to get yourself a room somewhere near where you work. It'll work out fine that way. You can still come and see me."

Fuoss sat stiffly, looking at the opposite wall over her shoulder. "Sure. Sure, Carol. I understand. It'll work out pretty well." He tightened his arms around her. "I'll find a good job for the Winter, and then maybe we can really set up something in style."

"I'd like that, Stac," she murmured in his ear. She drew her head back and kissed him. "I like you, Stac. You know I do. It just doesn't work out right now. You know that."

"Sure."

He moved to a furnished room in New Hyde Park, and rode the bus a mile up to work for ten days. He wrote Carol a few letters, and got a few answers. He read the paper one day and saw that Operation Spaceward had officially begun. Stock in Androids Incorporated, DuPont, and General Aniline went up again. Tal Cummins was getting his, but the androids —*we're getting ours, too.*

On Friday, the fourteenth of August and the thirteenth day of his last two weeks, he went out to Babylon with his crew.

They dug a hole two yards deep and about five across for an oak the owner wanted moved into it. They cut a ramp into one side of the hole, and craned the tree over to the top of the ramp. A bunch of overhead wires that couldn't be cut or moved kept them from dropping the tree in, so they mounted it upright on a skid, lashed the tree firmly, and guyed it to the front bumper of a truck with a couple of lengths of Manila.

Stac was driving the truck. As the rest of the crew manhandled the tree over the lip of the ramp, he was supposed to lower it slowly, keeping the truck in double-low and judging the strain on the Manila.

It didn't work out that way. The Manila snapped, lashed a couple of boys across the face, and fouled the skid. The tree tipped forward, picked up momentum, and toppled over, catching a man under the branches.

Stac got out of the truck and the Boss came over to him.

"You stupid son-of-a-bitch!" the Boss said. "You stupid *android* son-of-a-bitch! I should have had more sense than to hire a ——!"

It was the first time Stac had heard the word, but it was

self-explanatory. It described in a simple term the substances from which they claimed androids were made.

Fuoss reached out and gathered the Boss's shirt up in his hands. "I ought to hit you," he said. "I ought to rub your face on a macadam road and drive a truck over your crotch."

The Boss turned pale. He saw the look on Fuoss's face. "You're nuts! " he screamed.

Fuoss laughed and pushed him away. "Yeah."

He had done it so many times that the blanket's constriction was nothing new. His arms flailed and his pillow fell to the floor, knocking the bottle over.

Woman.

Stac—little Stac, his firstborn. Have a cigar, Brownie. Have a cigar, you smug bastard. Good cigar, Brownie—nothing's too good for the first born. Have a fat cigar.

Woman. The woman raised her face.

Carol. *Carol!*

The Boss said: Get the hell away from her, you second-hand son of a . . .

Carol said: You second-hand son of a . . .

Little Stac said: You second-hand son of a son of a son of a sonofasonofasonofa . . .

He went out in the morning and bought another bottle. He went into the candy store next door for a pack of cigarettes, and then he went back to the liquor store and bought another bottle to make sure.

CHAPTER III

He looked at his watch. 2:30 Sunday morning, but still Saturday night, by almost anybody's definition. He moved his feet impatiently on the bed.

The door to the apartment opened, and Carol came in. There was a man with her.

"Go home, Brownie. Go home to your wife and your first-born son."

"God! What's keeping him on his feet!"

"Never mind what's keeping me on my feet, Brownie. Go home."

Brownfield left. "I'll call the police for you, Carol."

"Are you crazy? He's all right—he's just packaged. I've seen him like this before. You know—he's right. Go home to your wife. I'll take care of him."

"Well, all right."

"You bet it's all right. Now beat it." Fuoss locked the door behind him, turned around and leaned against it.

"Hi, Carol."

She smiled hesitantly. "Hi, Stac."

"Marry me, Carol?"

"Not right now, Stac. It's kind of late. Why don't you sack out and we can talk about it in the morning."

"Uh-uh. This morning business doesn't go. You gonna marry me?"

"Look Stac, fun's fun, and drinking's drinking, but there's a limit. I'm not sure I even want you to sleep here. There's a hotel down the block. Stay there and I'll see you in the morning."

"Can't stay at any hotel. Haven't got any more money. I had some in my topcoat pocket, but you took it."

"I didn't take it. There wasn't any there. You took every cent you had to the Island with you."

"You took it all right. But that's okay. I'll forgive you. Just marry me."

Carol moved around to the other side of an easy chair. "What are you talking about? Me, marry an android?"

"Listen, Carol. You've got to do it. Nobody's ever tried it before. Maybe there's a chance."

"A chance for what?"

Fuoss spread his arms pleadingly. "For Stac—for little Stac. We've got to try it, Carol. Please. Marry me, Lisa, please."

"My name isn't Lisa! You're crazy, you're raving nuts. Get the hell out of here!" She picked up a bookend. "You're insane!"

Fuoss picked up the Scotch bottle from the table beside the

door and broke the end off over the table's corner. He laughed. "Yeah."

Tal Cummins went hurriedly down the corridor between the cells. He was sweating, and his hair was not combed.

"There he is. You want to go in there?" The turnkey had stopped at Fuoss's cell.

"No, thanks." Cummins leaned forward and looked at Fuoss. "Stac?"

Fuoss looked up.

"You realize what you've done?" Cummins was suddenly shouting, waving the full-color newspaper in his hand. "You're all over the papers. The public's going crazy for your blood. You realize what you've done to the whole android re-establishment program?"

Fuoss got up and put his face close to Cummins. He looked into the lawyer's eyes. His hands wrapped around the bars.

"Is she dead?" he asked hopefully.

THE PEASANT GIRL

CHAPTER I

Because one of its two people had stopped living there during the night, the house was smaller the following morning. So it was a cottage door that Henry Spar closed behind him, just an hour past dawn. He looked at the low roof and the clapboarding which no rain had ever touched, and which was nevertheless just weatherworn enough. The cottage looked snug—comfortable to live in.

Henry's thin-set lips moved with quick pain. "Might of waited a decent time," he grunted at the sky.

The windowshades pulled themselves shut. Henry picked up

the scuffed suitcase between his feet and walked away, his head down.

He stood patiently waiting for the bus to come. His long, boney face held no expression, and neither did his eyes. His thin, graying hair was plastered across his narrow skull, and was still damp, cleanly furrowed by his comb. Once he raised his hand to scratch his scalp, but caught himself.

He was wearing his best suit. The cloth was still warm from the careful pressing he'd just given it. He looked down at his shoes, raised his feet one at a time, and rubbed them free of dust against his calves. Then he beat the backs of his pant legs with a few strokes of his big hands. After that, he stood without moving, the suitcase sitting and waiting beside him.

The bus came down the street on schedule, and Henry saw it wasn't any bigger than a coupé this morning—just room for him and the driver. This early in the day, the dispatcher mustn't have seen any other passengers waiting.

When the bus pulled up, Henry stopped, lifted the suitcase, and got in. He nodded to the driver, whom he knew pretty well, and sat looking straight out through the windshield, pulling up on his pants to save the crease over the knees. He didn't feel like talking.

The driver did, though. He touched the shift, set the autopilot for New York City, relaxed, and half-turned in the seat.

"Got me up pretty early today, Henry," he said. "What's taking you into the big town?"

Henry grunted without turning his head. The driver waited a minute, and then tried again.

"Never figured I'd see the day Henry Spar wasn't satisfied to stay in the town he was born in."

A stubborn twist set itself into Henry's mouth. He knew better than the driver just how uneasy he was about going into town for the first time in his life. Be different if he was a young buck, itching to cut loose a little. But the way it was, with him pretty fixed in his ways, you could expect trouble. And the driver didn't have any business talking about it.

"Shoppin' trip, Henry?"

Henry closed up one of his big-knuckled hands. "Dispatcher didn't tell you, huh?" he said bitterly.

The driver looked surprised. "Shuh, Henry, *he* doesn't know! All he's interested in is who's goin' where and when, not why."

"Think so, huh?" Henry asked, getting mad. "He looks in my head and he finds out all that, but he doesn't look for anything else. That what you're trying to tell me?"

The driver frowned and sighed. He held out a pack of cigarettes. "Smoke? Okay, please yourself.

"Something bothering you bad, Henry? Dispatcher isn't a bad guy. I never ran across a nasty one of them yet." The driver waited, and the cigarette lit up. Nobody knew for sure how that happened; it didn't matter much, as long as they lit.

The driver went on. "You've gotta look at it their way. They're like a guy with extra-good eyes. He can't help seein' farther than most people. What do you want him to do—put his eyes out so you won't feel bad? They can't keep from usin' what they got. Maybe they don't even much enjoy wet-nursin' us? Ever think of that? Maybe you ought to be kind of glad they're willin' to bother with us at all, instead of just letting us go hang?"

Henry turned his head toward the driver so fast that his hair shook out of place.

"I come home last night, and my sister wasn't there. Right in the midde of making dinner, by the looks of it, and they took her. Pot on the stove, bread on the board, waitin' to be sliced."

The driver's face twitched. His cheeks jumped in a quick wince of sympathy.

"Just you and your sister livin' there, wasn't it?" he asked soberly. "Name of Dorothy."

Henry nodded. He had his right hand held tight over his left, as if he was favoring a hurt.

The driver looked at the highway for a minute or two before he turned back to Henry. "Took her into Albany a couple of times, shopping. She was growin' up into a real woman."

He looked back at the road. "You might of expected it," he said in a quiet voice.

Henry nodded again, slowly. "I might of. Guess I did. But I kept hopin' they wouldn't notice her for a while yet."

"You know better'n that, Henry. They notice."

Henry looked down at the suitcase he'd kept in his lap instead of putting it in the back. "I know. But you don't figure that way until it happens." He shrugged in bewilderment. "I figured maybe they wouldn't take her at all. She wasn't what you'd call a real pretty girl. Favored Pap too much."

The driver shook his head.

Henry sighed. "I know. I know—don't seem to make much difference to them, one way or the other." He shifted in his seat. "They just take 'em. Woman can be talking to you, or cooking your supper, or walking down the street—one minute she's there, the next she's gone; they've took her." He talked in a dull voice, holding his hands tight together.

"I notice they don't break up any families," the driver said.

"What's your name for me and Dorothy?"

"Well—you know what I mean, Henry. It's not the same, a bachelor and his sister. You can take care of yourself. It's not like they left any kids without somebody to look after 'em, or anything like that."

"I'm going looking for her," Henry said with a sudden blunt note in his voice.

The driver stared at him. "*That* what you're goin' in town for?"

Henry moved his jaw forward. "That's right." He curled his left hand into a fist inside his right. "Going to ask the head one whether he knows who's got her."

The driver shook his head in complete amazement. "That don't make *sense*, Henry! You think they're gonna talk to you? You think one of *them* is gonna bother explainin' anything to one of *us*? Good Gosh, man, you're lucky they dispatched this bus for you! Shuh, what makes you think they're gonna tell you the truth in the first place?"

The driver put his hand up to touch Henry on the shoulder, and then pulled it back before he reached. "She might come home. Sometimes they do. I've heard about it happening. Why don't you just stay home and wait for her?"

Henry reached down and held the handle of the suitcase with all his other clothes and his woodworking chisels in it.

"Can't do that," he said to the driver. "I know what they are. I know they're boss. One of us can't do anything but ask 'em nice for a favor. Maybe I just been livin' in one little town all my life and not paying any mind to any business but what was mine. Maybe I ain't so sure of what I'm doing. But you got any women in your family?"

The driver's eyes fell, and he dropped his cigarette over the ashtray. It disappeared, and nobody knew for sure how that worked, either. It seemed kind of funny to suppose somebody did nothing but light cigarettes and empty ashtrays. "No, not me," the driver said. His voice had dropped. He looked out across the snub hood of the bus. "Courting always looked a little too uncertain, I guess. Besides, what's a man want with a family, these days?"

Henry looked at a roadsign they were going by. They were only another twenty minutes out of New York. He sat back with the suitcase held in his lap. His face went back to its stony calm, and his eyes focussed far ahead of the bus. "A man does what's right, not what's easy," he said.

CHAPTER II

Henry stepped out of the bus at Uptown Terminal in New York, and saw a man start walking toward him.

Henry watched carefully as the slim, clear-skinned figure came nearer. The man's suit wasn't any better than Henry's, and he didn't have any special look on his face. But you could tell.

Henry stood waiting, the suitcase between his feet. The bus began to pull away, and the driver stuck his head out through the side window. He flashed a nervous look at the man. "Well, good luck, Henry," he said uncomfortably.

"Thanks," Henry muttered without turning his head.

"Mr. Spar," the man said.

Henry waited. He'd never been this close to one of them that he knew of. They were all over, but this was the first one he could look at and know it for sure.

"You want to see Mr. Kennealy."

"That's the head man, huh?" It was tough, talking to one of them. Henry hadn't thought about it before, but it would be. You knew you didn't have to talk out loud, but knowing wasn't proof. You talked anyway, feeling like a damned fool, and you knew he knew how you felt. Only you hoped that maybe you were different—maybe you had an extra-thick skull, or something—and you knew he knew about that feeling, too.

"No," the slim fellow answered. "But Mr. Kennealy can answer your questions for you." There was a funny, embarrassed kind of look on his face.

"How about you doing it?" Henry said. "You got 'em all figured out, don't you?" His hands were closed stiffly at his sides. He knew the messenger could look inside his head and see the way he felt. But it didn't do a man any good to just think mad. He had to act it, too.

The messenger stopped, as if he was trying to find the right words. "I'm sorry. Mr. Kennealy is the man to see. I'm on permanent assignment here as an advisor to visitors. I'm restricted to performing that service," he tacked on.

Henry hefted his suitcase. "If you're plannin' to pass me around from man to man, forget it. I come to stay until I get my sister or you send me back. If you're gonna give in at all, do it now, or get rid of me fast. Nothing I can do about that, I guess."

The messenger's face turned red at the cheeks. "I'm sorry, Mr. Spar," he said awkwardly. "But I can only refer you to Mr. Kennealy. Believe me, Mr. Spar," he went on earnestly, "there's no reason for you to be suspicious of our motives."

Henry grunted. The messenger sighed and spread his hands. "There's no way to convince you of the truth, is there?" he said. He sounded like he wasn't used to the idea.

Henry just looked at him. Then pushed his jaw forward.

"All right," he said, "no sense wasting our time. How do I get to this Kennealy fellow?"

The messenger looked relieved, but his voice was still troubled. "We have a car waiting for you. Right over here."

"Waitin' for me, huh?" Henry frowned. They had the skids all greased ahead of time. "How come a car, if you fellows are so almighty powerful?"

The messenger opened the door for him. There was even a driver. Henry couldn't make out whether he was another one of them or not. "You might not like it, Mr. Spar."

Henry climbed in. Maybe not. But you wouldn't figure they'd care, one way or the other. These people didn't have to answer to any man for the things they did. It had to figure they had some mighty good reason for being so polite to somebody who wasn't anything but a pretty fair cabinetmaker.

"All right, Simmons," the messenger told the driver. He took his hand off the door. "Goodbye, Mr. Spar."

"So long," Henry said grudgingly, and the car rolled down a ramp and out of the busy terminal. They went past the other section, and he saw their travelers coming in, suddenly turning up on numbered platforms, getting their local bearings, and going out again.

He looked at the back of the driver's neck. "You one of them?" he asked.

The driver nodded without turning around. "That's right, Mr. Spar. I'm one of us."

CHAPTER III

He went through the door marked "Mr, Kennealy", and found himself standing in front of a desk with a big, shaggy looking man behind it. Henry put his suitcase down.

"Hello, Mr. Spar," the man said. "I'm Matt Kennealy. Have a seat." Henry looked over to one side, and there was a chair, looking old and comfortable, still rocking a little bit in its hangers from coming out of wherever Kennealy'd got it. Henry brought his suitcase over to it and sat down.

You could tell this Kennealy was a boss. Whatever it was that made you recognize his kind in the first place, he had about twice as much of it as the young one down at the depot.

"Have a comfortable trip down?" he asked.

Henry gave him a sour look. "Let's not play around the bush, Mr. Kennealy."

Kennealy looked down at his thick-fingered hands, that were playing with a letter-opener.

"Just trying to be polite, Mr. Spar," he said in a voice that, for all it was deeper and surer of itself, reminded Henry of the young one down at the depot, even though the two of them didn't look one bit alike.

"Well, you can see I ain't in the mood for it," Henry said. "Sorry about it, but that's the way it is," he added. He didn't like talking to people like this. People or anybody.

Kennealy was nodding to himself. "Yes, I *could* see," he admitted. "But I didn't. I *was* being polite, Mr. Spar."

Henry looked at him angrily. "Even if it was true—what makes you think any of us would believe you? If you can see into our heads, you can see in all the time. So why don't you stop this off-again, on-again stuff? You're better'n us, and I guess we'll all admit it. So either run us or don't—suit yourself, but don't try and have it both ways. Where's Dorothy?" He clenched his hands down over his knees and looked at Kennealy stone-faced. He hadn't meant to come out at him that way, but now he'd done it he had to go on. He thought about Dorothy, and the way they might be treating her.

Kennealy's face turned red as soon as Henry thought of that. His eyes dropped and he fumbled with the letter-opener.

"No . . ." he mumbled after a while, "you're wrong."

Henry settled back in his chair and folded his arms. He guessed the look on his face was answer enough to that. Even if this wasn't one of the people who didn't need words to be talked to.

Kennealy got his upper lip between his teeth and worried at it for a minute.

"You don't know much about us, Mr. Spar."

"I keep to myself."

"Mr. Spar, we try not to disturb your people's lives, too. We do as much as we can to let you live the way you're accustomed to."

"It don't look that way to me, Mr. Kennealy."

Kennealy spread his hands out flat on his desk blotter and looked down somewhere near them. "I know. It can't be helped. If we didn't try, Lord knows what would happen between your people and ourselves. But when we do, both sides know it's just a joke." He shook his head and sighed. "It can't be helped," he said again. He looked up. "Mr. Spar, I haven't had any practice in being tactful. This isn't my regular job. Dorothy's with my son."

Henry didn't say anything for a long time. His eyes got a bland and far-off look in them.

It was hard to think of. He'd raised Dorothy ever since she was five. There was twenty years' age between them—in some ways, she was more like his daughter. That didn't matter so much. He'd feel the same way if it happened to any young girl he knew. Maybe he wouldn't go looking for her—it wouldn't be his duty. But he'd feel the same way.

"I wanted to talk to you first, Mr. Spar," Kennealy said into the quiet. "As the groom's father."

Henry lifted his head up. "They married?"

Kennealy's face turned red again, but this time he was mad. "What did you expect?" he barked. His heavy shoulders hunched up under his coat. "What kind of a—" He stopped, shook his head, and cleared his face up. "Never mind," he said in a quiet voice. "I know what kind of a mind you've got. I don't blame you for not seeing things clearly, under the circumstances."

"Meaning what?"

Kennealy took a deep breath. "Mr. Spar, we're human beings. We laugh and cry. We raise our children, too. If that sounds foolish to you, I can't help it."

Kennealy leaned forward. He said each word as if it was the most important one in the world.

"We came out of your stock—and not so long ago. We're not something that dropped out of the sky or burst out of the ground. We've got ten thousand years of the same culture behind us. We've got the same history—the same forefathers; the same traditions; the same roots. We have nothing of our own. We have only our human past, and our human natures. You're the ones who see us as a separate race. We don't. We can't.

"We look back, and see ourselves as a part of the same human racial tree. We can trace ourselves back to the same proliferating ooze that you can. But you look across, and see only a new branch, standing away from you, and you say we're different —we're separate.

"Well, Mr. Spar, we're 'them', we're 'the other ones', to you. You haven't given us a distinct name, and Lord knows we can't think of one either; we don't want to, and maybe, deep underneath, you know better, too."

Kennealy looked across the room at Henry, and you could see he was getting mad again.

"I raised my boy the way you would have. I watched him walk for the first time—does it make any difference whether he did it on his feet or some other way? I sent him to school. I played with him. I wanted him to marry a girl I'd be proud to call my daughter. He did."

Kennealy beat his heavy hands together. "If I was one of you, and you came to me saying the things you've been thinking about my son and your daughter, I'd punch you in the mouth."

"Well, come ahead," Henry said tightly, getting up.

Kennealy waved him back. "Oh, sit down, will you!"

Henry stuck his jaw out. "No! Be damned if I do. You want to fight, come ahead."

Kennealy's eyes turned a smokey red. His face got tight. "*Sit down!*" Something rammed into Henry's chest and shoved him down in the chair.

"And you can claim foul all you want to," Kennealy growled. He got up and paced back and forth behind the desk. "I've tried to keep it decent," he muttered, looking as mad at himself as he was at Henry. "The kids deserve a close-knit family behind them." He stopped suddenly and looked at Henry.

"Look—I'm sorry. I've got a rough temper. It's the Irish in me. I didn't want to start anything. I figured we might even wind this up by shaking hands." He looked at Henry again and shrugged his bulky shoulders. "Okay, I've spoiled that. And you're no help, either."

He sat down. "Okay. We're at loggerheads good and proper. Suppose you go down and see the kids. They're in Trenton. You want to go?"

Henry looked at him with his hands curled up into knobby fists.

"All right," Kennealy said. "So you *don't* have to talk. Okay. The car's downstairs. Simmons'll take you down to the station."

Henry stood up and lifted his suitcase. He looked hard at Kennealy. "What're you gonna do if I take Dorothy back with me? You gonna let me?"

Kennealy shrugged, his eyes looking sad. "I don't know," he sighed. "It depends. Find out for yourself." He picked up the letter-opener and stabbed it deep into the desk. As soon as he pulled it out the wood closed up, and he stabbed it in again. "We would have talked to you first, if we could have, you know." He looked up. "Good luck."

"Thanks, Mr. Kennealy," Henry said, his thin mouth twisted up at one corner. He wondered how many of them had been listening in, and he wondered what they thought. They knew what he was thinking.

He walked out of Kennealy's office with his suitcase bumping against his leg.

He settled down in the plush-covered seat of the old coach, and put the suitcase on the floor beside him, setting it so it wouldn't fall over.

The conductor came down the aisle, collecting tickets. Henry held his out, but the conductor shook his head. "That's all right. Save it. Mr. Kennealy's compliments."

Henry knew the conductor couldn't help it, but he got mad anyway. There wasn't any other way he could take it out. He slapped the ticket into the conductor's hand and sat facing front, his eyes feeling hot, as the train moved out of the station.

CHAPTER IV

As soon as the train got all the way over the bridge into New Jersey, it began to change. Henry'd heard stories about it, but he hadn't taken much stock in it. When the windows began to run and turn colors, and the floor and ceiling sagged down and heaved upward, he had to hang on to the arms of his seat and close up his eyes. He felt the cloth change texture under his hands, and then it was all over. The windows were wide and crystal-clear, running one solid pane the length of the car. There were fluorescent panels in the chrome-trimmed ceiling, and the floor was some sort of shiny composition tile. The seats were foam slabs lying in chrome trays. Henry looked ahead, at a curve in the roadbed, and he could see that the train was a long, flex-jointed streamlined cylinder, running on a single rail set in a trough.

The man in the seat behind him chuckled, and Henry turned his head around.

"Somethin' funny, Mister?"

The man cut his laugh off. "I guess not, if that's the way you feel," he said. He stuck out his hand. "My name's Charlie Hopkins. Representing the Allied Novelty line—pen and pencil sets."

Henry shook his hand and let it go.

"I do a lot of traveling," the salesman said. "I'm used to it. Guess you're not. It happens every time you cross a state line—oftener, sometimes," he explained. "Depends on how people feel. Now, up here in this end of Jersey, they're all for progress and being modern. Look out at those factories."

Henry looked through the window. The train was running between a refinery and a chemical works. Everything was shiny chrome and colored plastic panels. Everything gleamed; the smoke and fumes pouring out of the chimney pots was disappearing as soon as it hit the air.

"Now, out in the Middlewest, they've got stretches where one town's just like another: old houses, lawns, trees along the streets, old drugstore with a marbletop soda fountain and wire chairs. One town after another, just exactly the same as the last. Only the names're different, and even they've got the same sound to them. I still get confused.

"Sorry if I made you mad, laughing at you. I was just thinking back to the first time it happened to me. It's sort of a gag around the office, you see? They send you out—and they don't tell you. Man, when I felt my seat melting under me, I thought I was dead and in Hell. I came near to—"

Henry grunted and turned back around. He closed down tight on his teeth.

They could do anything they wanted to. They had the whole world to fool around with—and the people in it, too, who couldn't help themselves. They could rip the roof off from over your head, and pick you up and set you down somewheres else. They could be a thousand miles away and know what was in your head. They could take the girl you'd raised from a child—without asking; without a sign or a sound, except for a knife suddenly dropping on the breadboard in an empty house.

He got off the train at Trenton, put his suitcase down on the platform, and waited while the train pulled out. He knew his hair was mussed up, and his suit had wrinkles in it, but they could just stay that way. When he saw Dorothy waiting on the other side of the right-of-way with a young fellow that must be Kennealy's boy, he picked up his suitcase and walked through the underpass. He put his feet down hard on each of the steps up to the other platform, and when he got to Dorothy and the boy he just dropped his bag with a thump and waited for somebody else to start talking.

Up close, he could see that Dorothy was looking prettier than she ever had in her life. She had a dress made out of some kind of pale blue material that brightened up her hair color just enough so it looked like a good blonde. It did something to her eyebrows, too, and her eyes, he guessed. She was looking straight at him, with her chin pushing forward, and you somehow didn't much notice that thinness to her nose unless you knew to look for it. She had her hair combed in some fancy way that showed off the good shape to her head, and she was wearing lip rouge.

He looked at Kennealy's boy. He looked too much like his father to be handsome. He hadn't put on the weight yet, but he had the big, flat-looking nose and the oversize ears. He looked a little worried, but he wasn't ashamed, or scared.

"Hello, Henry," Dorothy said, sounding a little uncertain, too, but calm under it. She took hold of the boy's hand. "Henry, this is Tom. We got married late yesterday afternoon. We wanted to tell you, but I knew how you'd act about it."

"How are you, Mr. Spar," Tom Kennealy said, holding out his hand.

Henry looked at the hand for a minute, but he wound up taking it. He looked at Dorothy. "So that's the way it is. I thought maybe his father was lyin' to me."

Tom's face got an angry look to it for a minute, but he held his temper in.

"Henry," Dorothy said, "I'd appreciate it if you were polite." She pushed her chin forward a little more. "I can see your side of it, but there's ours, too."

"Maybe," Henry grunted. He looked at the Kennealy boy again. "Maybe it might of been more polite for you to come and talk to me, if you had your eye on Dorothy."

"Mr. Spar, she was already gone. And she's already told you she knew what you'd say."

"Already gone, huh? Just like that. You reach out and grab her; pull her out of her home and bring her down here. And then you say 'Darling, will you marry me?' and the next day you're married and you figure it might be nice to tell her brother. Is that it?"

Tom Kennealy got that uncomfortable look in his eyes that his father and the messenger at the depot had.

"Mr. Spar, anything can sound bad if you want it to. I didn't kidnap Dorothy; anyway, I didn't plan it or do it deliberately. It wasn't down here that I brought her, by the way. It was England. I was working on a paper at Oxford. My mother lives here."

Henry felt his big fingers curling. "Didn't do it deliberately, huh?" he said in a tight-throated voice. "I guess she went to Oxford, England, of her own free will?"

"No, I didn't, Henry," Dorothy said, just as stubborn as he was. "But I stayed of my own free will. I didn't have to be with Tom very long before I knew I wanted to." She looked Henry square in the eyes. "A woman knows her proper man, Henry. And don't you think different." She reached over and took the Kennealy boy's hand again, holding it tight.

"We don't have waiting periods, Mr. Spar," Tom Kennealy said. "We don't get married unless we're sure it's right."

"And you're sure, huh? Well, I guess so. And I guess she can read your mind, too? She can be just as sure?" Henry felt his teeth settling hard against each other.

Dorothy pushed herself forward and faced him up close. Her eyes were snapping like a whip. "Henry, that's enough of that! You can't take care of me forever. You can't keep me in the house until it's too late for me and all I'm good for is to be your housekeeper. How many boys are there back home who were courting me? You've got to be like . . . like Cleopatra before they'll even speak to you." Dorothy put her foot down hard on the platform. "You know where we got married? In Scotland, that's where. In a little church with the mist over the sea and the sun just breaking through. When was I ever in Scotland, Henry? Or when did I hope to go? And we're going to Hawaii tonight; and this is a Paris gown—and a man in Rome did my hair this morning."

"That's a good price, I guess," Henry said.

Dorothy took a step back. Her face went pale for a minute, and then her mouth went thin and bitter. She looked at Henry like he was something she didn't recognize.

"Mr. Spar," Tom Kennealy growled.

"Yeh?"

"Mr. Spar, I know for a fact that Dorothy doesn't give a darn about any clothes or hair-dos." Young Kennealy's jaw was white at the corners, but his eyes were hurt looking. He was holding his temper down as best he could. Henry guessed the boy thought there was something more important to get across. He waited.

"Mr. Spar, I *know* Dorothy's in love with me."

"Sure. And the minute I can read *your* mind, I'll believe you. Maybe I'll even decide she means something to you."

"At this point, I don't care whether you do or not, frankly," Kennealy said, his voice as ready to break as a cable under strain. "But she means something to me. She's my wife. I married her. And I'm going to stay married to her. Look—if she'd eloped with some young buck in a tin lizzie, would you be acting like this toward her? I saw her. You know what happens then, Mr. Spar? To one of us? It's quicker than thought. I saw her, and she was there. In England. With me. I've seen my share of women. This was the only one I wanted. So there she was. And I was lucky—she didn't want to go back. And she would have, if she wanted to. What makes you think we haven't got laws? What makes you think that with each of us having a million minds looking into his own, we can possibly have criminals or psychotics? If she hadn't wanted to stay, she wouldn't be here—she'd be back home with you, darning your socks."

Henry looked at Dorothy, but she wouldn't even look at him.

"All right," he said, looking back to Tom Kennealy. "You're boss." He picked up his suitcase and turned away. "You can come back home whenever you want," he said to Dorothy and went down to wait for the train back.

He found out he'd rather get off the train in Jersey City and walk across the bridge into New York, but that was about all. He turned up back in his cottage the next morning, and nobody thought anything much of it. He went to work in the shop, and got docked a day's pay for being out. Nobody talked about Dorothy. They didn't make any point of not talking about her. They just didn't, and after a while Henry stopped noticing it. He settled down to his work, and made his own bed and cooked his own breakfasts.

CHAPTER V

One day the house got bigger again. When there was a knock on the door, later that night, he just opened it and stood in the doorway, with the light streaming out from behind him and over Matt and Tom Kennealy, along with Dorothy.

"Hello, Mr. Spar," Matt Kennealy said.

Henry nodded. "Come in. I can't stop you. It's no surprise. I saw the nursery."

Dorothy kept her arms tight around the blanket-wrapped bundle in her arms. She looked worried, but under that she looked fine. Her face had rounded a little, and the little pinches over the bridge of her nose were gone. She came close to being beautiful.

"Thanks, Mr. Spar," Matt Kennealy said. "But we can't stay. It isn't comfortable." He shrugged his shoulders and grinned a little. "Both of us came down with Dorothy because Tom doesn't know how to drive a car." He grinned again and shook his head. "It's always the same. Babies don't like change. They want things exactly the way they are. This one's as stubborn as they come. He doesn't mind riding in a car—that's not what he considers a change. But he kicks up the very devil of a fuss if Tom or I try to so much as look around while we're near him. That makes Junior see things he's not ready for—so he deafens everybody for miles around with a yell that you *can* hear in Madagascar, if you're listening for it."

Dorothy came into the doorway. She smiled at Henry. "You've got quite a nephew, Henry. They tell me there's nothing special about him, but I've got my doubts. Anybody with Tom's temper and Pap's stubbornness in him can't be just ordinary."

Henry didn't smile back, and after a little while Dorothy's face went back to its worried look. "I'd like to stay here with you until he's grown up enough," she said.

Henry grunted. "Go or stay. Nothin' I got to say about it. What's the boy's name?"

"Billy."

"Billy, huh? Guess it's a good one. I saw your clothes and stuff in the bedroom next to the nursery. Must have figured I'd let you."

"We can take it out again, Henry," Dorothy said.

He shook his head. "No. No, I told you you could come home."

"Thank you."

"Half of what's mine is yours. Nothing to be thankful for." He turned around and went back to his chair beside the fireplace, facing away from the doorway.

He heard Dorothy kiss her husband. "Good night, Tom."

"Good night, Honey. See you tomorrow?"

"I don't know. Better give me a day to get settled. Make it the day after."

"All right. I'll miss you."

"I'll miss *you*. Now you'd better be getting back—you've got at least four miles of road to cover before you're out of our offspring's range." She laughed softly, and Tom and Matt both chuckled with her.

"Good night, Dorothy," Matt Kennealy said.

"Good night, Dad. I hope your driving improves with practice."

There was another general chuckle.

"Good night, Mr. Spar," Matt Kennealy said.

Henry grunted an answer. There was a minute's quiet, and then Henry heard Matt sigh, and mutter something annoyed. But after a minute the door closed, and Dorothy came into the room, carrying the boy. She sat down opposite him, and looked into the fire.

Henry picked up the paper and started reading it.

"Anything to say, Henry?" Dorothy asked after a while.

Henry looked up. "That's a pretty coat," he said, and went back to reading.

At breakfast the next day, he looked down at his plate. "What's that?"

"Scrambled eggs and onions," Dorothy said. "It's good."

He took a sip of his coffee. "Pick up anything else from being around them?"

She took a slow breath. "A few things." She moved her fork around on her plate.

"You've got the sound of a city woman to your talk, I notice. I suppose you know a whole string of foreign languages, too, with all that traveling?"

Her mouth was drawing out slowly, getting thin and tight. "A little of some. Tom does most of the talking when we need it. I'm still learning."

"Learn how to look inside his head, yet?" He watched her closely.

Her hand closed down hard on the fork. "As much as any married woman with her husband." She looked up, the anger showing plain in her eyes. "Maybe a little more. One of us can do a few things, if she's shown how." She put her fork down. "Henry," she said, "we're going to be living more or less in the same house for the next five years, at least. Maybe we won't—maybe I made a mistake in coming back. But I'm here to try it. Don't make it harder on yourself than it has to be."

Henry shrugged, feeling a shadowy kind of a disappointment inside him. She'd made it plain enough, but he'd been hoping she'd maybe wanted to come back because she saw she was wrong.

"Not gonna be hard on me at all," he said. "You go your way, I'll go mine."

"That's the way you feel."

"That's it." He pushed the plate aside without touching the eggs, got up, and left the house to go down to the shop.

A few days a week, he slept in the room next to the nursery, minding the boy while Dorothy was away. He went with her once, after hiring a woman to come over, when she took the bus out to the crossroads near Aitken's Hill. He'd watched her climb up it in the twilight, and stand at the top. Then she was gone, and an early star shone through the place where she'd been standing. He'd waited until she came back, hours later, looking rested and quiet, but he'd never gone again. And that was the way they slowly settled down to living. And a few years went by.

There were books in the house, and Dorothy got a music player. He didn't read the books. He had to hear the music, sometimes—he got to like some of it—but he didn't know how to work the player and didn't want to.

The boy grew. He was quiet for a long time. Dorothy said he was learning to talk. And after that he started coming and going around the house. He never went too far, because he didn't know his bearings for very many places, and Henry got used to having him turn up in odd corners.

Then he learned to speak. He sounded like Henry sometimes, and sometimes like Dorothy, at first, but after a while he smoothed out and sounded like somebody in his own right.

Dorothy stopped having to go out to the hill before Tom could reach her, but still went out to see him, and that was fine with Henry.

And one day, when Henry was down in the basement, working on a new chiffonier for one of the bedrooms, the boy turned up beside him and stood watching.

Henry didn't mind. He kept on planing the leg he was working on, feeling the blade cut smoothly through the maple. Then he set it up on the lathe and laid out his chisels.

"Ever see this before, Boy?"

Billy shook his head. "Never watched before. Looks interesting."

Henry grunted. "Dunno if it's interestin' or not. I like it."

He switched the motor on, set his chisel solidly on the T, and made his first cut. Working carefully, he rounded the end eight inches of the upright.

"That part's going to be the leg, huh? And the rest of it's going to form one corner of the chiffonier," Billy said.

"You know as well as I do, Boy."

"Guess I do. Uncle Henry, can I have that piece of wood over there?"

Henry looked over. "That red one? No, Boy. That's mahogany. You don't want to fool with that—it's too good a piece of wood. Take that—"

Billy'd already picked up the piece of scrap pine. He looked at Henry, and carefully took the tools he knew it was all right to use.

That was one thing, anyway. He could know how to use tools, and there wasn't any trouble about him hurting himself. Henry forgot about him and went back to cutting out the leg.

After that, Billy was down in the shop a good deal of the time. It wasn't long before Henry trusted him with the lathe; it kept the boy out of trouble, and Dorothy didn't mind.

Billy didn't do much with it, though. He just turned wood into all kinds of shapes for a while. Henry decided it was just another way of playing, for a while, but after a month or so Billy began pestering him.

"Uncle Henry—what's wrong with this?"

He was holding up a wooden ball he'd turned. Henry grunted, put his paper down, and took the ball in his hands.

"Looks all right to me, Boy," he said. "Good job, matter of fact." It was as true as you'd want for freehand turning, and then some.

Billy shook his head. "It looks wrong. The way the grain runs."

"Well, that's something else, Boy." He'd turned it some funny cross-grained way.

So Henry taught him about grain. He showed him how to catch the flow of it in the shape of the wood—how to bring it out, and how to bury it. He taught him about finishing—about treating it so it wouldn't crack out as the piece dried. He taught him about how wood is alive a long time after it's out of the tree, and how you have to know which way it'll swell, and which way it'll shrink.

And when Billy asked if it was all right to use the piece of mahogany if he promised to replace it, Henry let him.

Dorothy came into the parlor. "Henry?"

"Yeh." He knocked the dottle out of his pipe into his palm, and dropped it into a wastebasket.

"Henry, look at this."

He grunted and looked up. She was holding a wooden shape in her hands. "Billy just gave me this."

Henry grunted. "Let's see it." Dorothy handed it to him.

It felt good in his hands. It was some kind of complicated shape that seemed to turn itself in his hands all by itself. It glowed with the soft amber color of beeswaxed mahogany. The tight grain shot through it, flowing in long bands along one surface, jabbing up under another. He set it down on a table under a lamp and turned it around slowly, and couldn't tell from the shape and shifting glow of it when he'd gotten back to his starting place. The shape just seemed to flow on and on.

Henry straightened up slowly. "Something," he said. "The boy's got a touch of something."

Dorothy picked the shape up in her hands and held it again. "It's more than just a touch, Henry. He came up to me and just handed it to me. He didn't make any fuss over it—but I could tell. This is what he wants to do."

"Don't see why not. He's got a good hand for wood. A man with a good, skilled hobby has something he can be proud of. The boy'd make a good man, down at the shop. But I don't suppose that's exactly what they have in mind for him." He gave her the bitter look that had been passing between them for years, now.

He saw it make her mouth thin out like it always did.

"This is more than a hobby," she said. She got suddenly angry, the way she did, sometimes.

"Henry, they don't have anything of their own. They don't have *anything*. They borrow it all from us, and try and make it do. They waste themselves keeping this world as close as possible to what we want. But what else can they do? They don't know what their kind of world should be, yet.

"Billy's the first one. You don't know how rare it is for one of them to know how to work with his hands—how to take something that's of the Earth and shape it so it points the way to wherever they're going. They didn't have that, up to now." She held the shape up. "This is the first thing they've ever made that's of themselves."

Henry's mouth jerked up at one corner. "You suppose now your Tom'll love you for sure, now?"

Dorothy looked like he'd hit her, for a minute. Then she looked at him, and he could tell by her face that she'd given up on something for the last time.

"There isn't any answer I can give you, is there?" she said in a low voice. "You're just going to be like that."

He grunted and walked into the living room. He picked up the paper and started reading it, the hard lines tight across his cheeks.

He stayed more or less like that for the rest of his life, his hair getting grayer and his hands getting knobbier. After Dorothy left with the boy, and the house became a cottage again, he took care of himself pretty well until he got too old. He'd learned to be pretty fond of the boy, but he never forgave Dorothy.

If you would like a complete catalogue of Quartet's publications please write to us at 27 Goodge Street, London W1P 1FD